Next
patient,
please

Dr Brijeshwar Singh is an orthopaedic surgeon, writer, poet and theatre impresario based in Bareilly, Uttar Pradesh. The patronage and promotion of theatre through the Rang Vinayak Rang Mandal theatre repertory and the annual theatre festival organized in Bareilly at the Windermere Theatre, which is owned and established by Dr Singh, earned him the Sangeet Natak Akademi award for 2020. His Daya Drishti Charitable Trust helps children born with thalassemia avail regular and life-saving transfusions. A writer in both Hindi and English, his story, 'Keh do Gunjan!' was published in *India Today*'s annual literature edition, 2019. This is his second book. Follow him at:

Twitter: @BrijeshwarS
Instagram: @drbrijeshwarsingh

Next patient, please

STORIES FROM
THE TRENCHES OF MEDICINE

DR BRIJESHWAR SINGH

RUPA

Published by
Rupa Publications India Pvt. Ltd 2022
7/16, Ansari Road, Daryaganj
New Delhi 110002

Sales centres:
Allahabad Bengaluru Chennai
Hyderabad Jaipur Kathmandu
Kolkata Mumbai

This is a work of fiction. Names, characters, places and incidents are either the product
of the author's imagination or are used fictitiously and any resemblance to any actual
person, living or dead, events or locales is entirely coincidental.

ISBN: 978-93-9091-858-4

First impression 2022

10 9 8 7 6 5 4 3 2 1

The moral right of the author has been asserted.

To
Samar and Shivani.

Samar's poetry has always inspired me to write stories from the heart. Shivani, who is a friend, helped me learn how to go out of the way to help the needy—inspiring me to go to any lengths to do so.

Contents

Foreword	*ix*
प्राक्कथन	*xiii*
Preface	*xv*
1. The Touch of a Doctor	1
2. Make it Happen	13
3. That Boy, Bhrungesh	17
4. No Place like Home	22
5. Bittersweet	26
6. 101 Not Out	30
7. Wish Upon a Star	32
8. Something Borrowed, Something Blue	36
9. No Strings Attached	39
10. Boon or Bane	44
11. Dare to Dream	48
12. God's Plan	51
13. Priceless	54
14. All About Time	57

15. Like a Butterfly   61

16. Poison Ivy   63

17. Reminiscence   65

18. Unordinary   67

19. The Little Man   70

20. Euphoria   72

21. The Hero Lies in You   74

22. Son   77

23. A Blessing   80

24. There for you   82

25. Call My Name   88

26. A Second Chance   90

27. Hope   93

28. The Show Must Go On   95

29. Road to Recovery   98

30. The Final Parting   102

31. Nothing Can Stop You Now   113

32. Ma   116

33. Guilty   122

34. Prelude   129

35. Gunjan   133

36. The Survivor's Lament   140

37. Annihilation   152

38. The Horrific Summer of 2020   165

Acknowledgments   179

Foreword

To make a name and place for yourself while fulfilling the ideals of a chosen profession, or to become the pride of that profession, is neither everyone's cup of tea nor everyone's fate. In the words of Jigar Moradabadi:

Allah agar taufeeq na de
Insaan ke bas ka kaam nahin
(It's not up to us humans, if it isn't willed by God)

I am looking at the book *Next Patient Please*. To describe it pithily, I am reminded of one of my own couplets:

Ajeeb dard ka rishta dikhayee deta hai
Ke har gum aashna apna dikhayee deta hai.
(What is this strange bond of pain I see around me?
Everyone who knows misery, I see as my own)

This is not just a collection of stories, but a series of larger-than-life tales that take the readers on a magical journey, making sure that their creative flight does not come to an end. The writing has a spellbinding effect—something that is rare nowadays.

Dr Brijeshwar is an artist first and foremost and everything else later. He beats like an aching heart in every word of his shared experience. That is why he has learnt to embrace a demanding profession such as medicine like a writer or storyteller. Amongst his incredible tales, there is a four-year-old child, unwilling to accept defeat in his battle to survive, and a ninety-eight-year-old courageous senior citizen, whose positive thoughts you can almost touch, thanks to Dr Brijeshwar's incredible skill. Apart from looking after his patients' ailments, he possesses the art of dealing with their turbulent psychology.

He turns to his experience as a surgeon to cater to bleeding cuts and bruises, even as he addresses psychological problems, helplessness and uncertainty among the ailing with his healing sympathy and hopeful empathy. It is as if his support becomes a part of addressing the ailment, and that is not easy. The ability to counter his patients' dark thoughts and show them the light of hope is not possible due to his professional prowess alone, but the compassionate aspects of his personality that play a major role in making this possible.

It is surprising how easily he converts despair into hope, failure into success and defeat into victory. He succeeds in creating a culture of healing that is exemplary and inspiring, albeit with the grace of the divine. I pray that this journey of multi-hued stories opens a passage of contemplation for others in this profession. That it is successful in proving that even though it is god who relieves us—humans—of our misery, it is also his blessings that make us worthy of credit by making us mediums of healing.

Dear doctor, *Next Patient, Please* should be followed by 'Next in Line, Please'.

Wasim Barelvi

December 2021

प्राक्कथन

किसी भी पेशे के आदर्शों को जीकर जगह बनाना, नाम कमाना या उस पेशे का गौरव बनना न हर एक के बस का है, न हर किसी का मुकद्दर। बकौल जिगर मुरादाबादीख़अल्लाह अगर तौफ़ीक न दे इंसान के बस का काम नहीं।

नेक्स्ट पेशेंट प्लीज मेरे सामने है। कम से कम शब्दों में इसे बयान करना चाहूं तो अपना ही एक शेर याद आता है–

अजीब दर्द का रिश्ता दिखाई देता है
के हर गमआशना अपना दिखाई देता है।

यह कहानियों का मजमुआ नहीं, हकीकत बयानियों का ऐसा सिलसिला है जो शुरू होता है तो पाठक को अपने जादूई बहाव में पैर जमाने तक की इजाजत नहीं देता। कम तहरीरें ऐसी पढ़ने में आई होंगी जिनकी वाकया बयानी के सहर ने इस तरह अपने प्रभाव में लिया हो। कुछ भी कहिये, एक बात तय है कि डॉक्टर ब्रिजेश्वर फनकार पहले हैं, बाकी सबकुछ बाद में। सिर से पैर तक दिले दर्दमंद की तरह धड़कते हैं अपनी तजर्बाबयानी के एक-एक शब्द में। इसीलिए वो डॉक्टरी जैसे हौसलाआजमा पेशे को भी कवि या कहानीकार की तरह

बरतने का राज पा गए हैं। इस अद्भुत वाकया बयानी के पात्रों में चार बरस का साहस प्रतीक बच्चा भी है जो शारीरिक बेसरो-सामानी के बावजूद संघर्ष की जंग हारने को तैयार नहीं और अट्ठानवै साल के जवाँहिम्मत बुजुर्ग भी, जिनकी सकारात्मक सोचों से संवाद करने की असाधारण क्षमता है डॉक्टर ब्रिजेश्वर के पास। वो रोगी की जाहिरी दशा के साथ उसकी मनोविज्ञानी उथलपुथल से भी रूबरू होने का हुनर जानते हैं।

खूँ रोती चोटों के लिए माहिर हाथों और ऑपरेशन के उपकरण गों का सहारा लेते हैं तो रोगी की नफ्सियाती उलझनों, बेबसी और बेयकीनी को अपनी मसीहाना हमदर्दी और आशामिजाज दर्दमंदी से कुछ ऐसा सहारा देते हैं जैसे रोगी के दुख का हिस्सा हों। और यह कोई आसान बात नहीं। मरीज के जहनी अंधेरों को उम्मीद की रोशनी से परिचित कराने में उनकी पेशावराना कारकर्दगी ही काम नहीं दिखाती, उनके व्यक्तित्व का गैरमामूली मानवीय पक्ष भी बड़ा रोल अदा करता है।

हैरत होती है कि वो किस तरह हँसते-खेलते निराशा को आशा, नाकामी को कामयाबी और हार को जीत में बदल देने का कारनामा अंजाम देते हैं और उपचार संस्कृति का वो इतिहास रच देने में सफल हो जाते हैं जो अनुकरणीय भी है और प्रेरणादायक भी, मगर है यह यकीनन किसी दैवीय शक्ति के वरदान का सदका।

मेरी दुआ है कि उनकी हजार रंग गाथा का यह सफर इस नोबल प्रोफेशन से जुड़े लोगों के लिए चिन्तन के नए द्वार खोले और यह साबित करने में सफल हो कि इंसानी दुख तो भगवान दूर करता है, मगर यह उसका करम है कि वो इसका श्रेय हमें माध्यम बनाकर दिला रहा है।

डियर डॉक्टर, *नेक्स्ट पेशेंट प्लीज* के बाद 'नेक्सट इन लाइन प्लीज'।

वसीम बरेलवी
दिसंबर 2021

Preface

Finding yourself in pain and overcoming it is the key to survival. That's what you will read in these stories inspired by real life.

People can easily lose themselves when they're hurt. That pain transcends the physical plane and goes beyond the need to heal. Bodies get wrecked, memories get scarred, friends lose interest and families fall apart. But the human instinct for survival endures. The ultimate act of heroism is to love yourself, despite everything.

Through these stories, I want to capture the essence of human convictions. The conviction that is needed to recover, to work and survive. Many people, when faced with a threat, instantly worry about their near and dear ones. That's the beauty of human nature. On the one hand we want to survive because it's our basic instinct, while on the other, we want to survive just so we can secure the survival of our bloodlines. In the end, it's all about survival of the fittest.

You are fittest when you have conquered all obstacles

and, accepted all your faults and flaws as experiences. They are a part of your history, the person you are.

As the South Korean rapper Kim Namjoon puts it, 'Maybe I made a mistake yesterday, but yesterday's me is still me. I am who I am today, with all my faults. Tomorrow I might be a tiny bit wiser, and that's me, too. These faults and mistakes are what I am, making up the brightest stars in the constellation of my life. I have come to love myself for who I was, who I am, and who I hope to become.'

The Japanese have a unique way of expressing this philosophy through art.

Kintsugi (金継ぎ, 'golden joinery'), is the Japanese art of fixing broken pottery with lacquer mixed with powdered gold or other precious metals. The process glorifies the flaws of a piece of pottery instead of hiding them. It showcases the article's unique history.

The pot still stands, despite the cracks, just like a person continues to stand despite the wounds. Suffering is an essential part of the human journey. Just like a crack in a pot signifies the strength of the clay, wounds signify the strength of human beings and their will to hold on. The scars we wear depict our unique history and the battles that we have fought. After all, what doesn't kill you, makes you stronger.

How people's lives and attitudes have changed because of a traumatic event is an integral part of my conversations with patients. And it's mesmerizing how patients often bare their souls to me, proving that humans are the most vulnerable in front their doctors.

The impact of the experience is what makes them

special—similar to Cain in the Hebrew Bible. When the Lord confronted Cain with the sin of murdering his brother Abel, the Lord put a mark on him. The reason that Cain was allowed to live at all was so that all humans would be warned of God's judgement on sin.

However, Hermann Hesse in *Demian*, postulates that Cain's mark is one of distinction rather than shame. People who wear their battle scars are the ones who have gone through challenging circumstances and come out victorious. The mark signifies their victory and, thus, makes them truly special.

The stories in this book are not just about the people who are broken or who have survived. They are not about those who may have chosen the wrong path, made a wrong decision, or who just stumbled down a path to their cruel fate. It's about those who chose to live in spite of all that, who embraced their fate and decided to make things better. You'll read about people who chose to work hard as opposed to those who couldn't; others who sacrificed themselves, their dreams, their ambitions, and some who were compelled to take life-altering decisions on behalf of others who couldn't.

There's more to these stories than mere words. They are rich in human desperation. Some stories have more than a single interpretation. A villain in my story might be a hero to you, just as an athlete might be a cripple in your story. All I urge is that you to explore each story and make it your own.

The Touch of a Doctor

At the age of 51, one does pause to reflect on the past and prepare for the future. If you were to ask me to define myself, I would find it very difficult to separate the doctor, the citizen and the artist in me. I am fortunate that my own growth and evolvement are linked to my profession. I am sensitive to the human stories and the narratives I have encountered at work. As a citizen, a doctor and a theatre person, I have had the privilege to interact with so many people and hear their stories. Each one, a different tale. I continue to be enriched by these stories just like the ones that I heard, and was fascinated by, in my childhood. From my mother's lullabies and stories, I moved on to reading and studying literature, and listening to music. Later, I pursued theatre in Bareilly with the same passion as I put into studying for my career in medicine. As a trusted orthopaedic-trauma surgeon, I have always wanted to share with the world outside what goes on in the inner world of medicine: The pain and pleasure of my patients, my colleagues and myself. I believe that the humane aspect of medical practice is the most empowering. In today's world of technology driven, cut-throat competition and great advancement in medical science, talking of the humane aspect of medicine may seem a dichotomy, or worse, a charade. But it is not so.

As a doctor, who is also a citizen, I am by 'oath' meant to heal wounds and not inflame passions in war and peace.

The larger truth is that in the philosophy of medicine, the bond between the doctor and patient is a profound narrative.

Let me herein give a summary of my own connect with medicine and my own evolution. I was born at Queen Mary Hospital in Lucknow. At the age of five, I encountered a severe medical challenge. I developed rheumatic poly-arthritis. This was a blessing in disguise. It neutralised my hyperactivity as a child. The extended bedrest not only helped me grow up, but also taught me to understand the problem. I was subjected to painful intramuscular injections. I hated Balrampur Hospital in Lucknow where I was routinely taken to receive these injections. What kept me going were the Burma Biscuit treats and the toys that my mother would bribe me with. I must hasten to add that in the course of my treatment at Balrampur Hospital I became very fond of my paediatrician, Dr Sheela. As a doctor, when I look back I can trace that, I made my first connect with the medical world and fraternity while lying in the hospital as a patient. A fair quotient of humanity got ingrained in me, not just genetically, but also through the tender care I received as a patient at the hospital. Another incident that I recall is of my father developing ulcers in his stomach. He would spend sleepless nights taking antacids.

When the problem got aggravated, Dr Kothiwal suggested gastrojejunostomy, which was then a popular surgery for ulcers. My father's hospitalisation, surgery and discharge was imprinted on my memory. Unlike most children, I was very fascinated by the process of my father's treatment and discharge from the hospital. This was the exact point of my emotional bonding and desire to be a doctor. My fascination for surgery life got its wings from the love and emotional security that I received during my childhood and youth. It taught me the humane values that a doctor most needs.

Initially, especially during my first year in medicine, I found the study of human medical science to be too clinical, confining and objective. I believed that beyond just the clinical the emotional quotient, a subjective and first-hand experience and reaction to life played the central part in determining human social behaviour. In my first year, I had opted for paediatrics. It was a half-hearted choice. However, this period turned out to be an amazing period in my life. It was here that I met the humblest clinician, someone who would exercise a profound influence on my own clinical practice in the future. I had joined my post-graduation without any clinical exposure to paediatrics. On the first day of my residency in a children's hospital, while undertaking my very first procedure, I was given the task of putting an intravenous (IV) catheter into a four-year-old thalassaemic boy. I had no experience. It was more challenging because the child's veins were choked. My initial attempts failed. I got nervous. My heartbeat increased. I heard a voice speaking softly, 'Give yourself permission to fail a few times. It is not the end of the world if you miss inserting an IV once.' It was the gentlest assurance and it came from Dr Khadwal, my senior resident doctor. I turned to her and said, 'Please help me through this ma'am, it is my first day and I have never before inserted an IV.' Dr Khadwal guided me step-by-step and gave me clarity on the process. As is the case with all the new doctors, my head was full of textbook knowledge. I was a timid learner who was hesitant to roll up his sleeves and examine a patient. Dr Khadwal was an experienced guide who knew all about the human body. She had performed hundreds of complicated procedures and could correctly deduce the symptoms of innumerable diseases. It was she who taught me what the touch of a doctor meant. She had a heart of gold. She helped patients by providing them with monetary aid out of her own salary. Dr Khadwal would give money to the junior doctors on duty to buy snacks for themselves. This was also to ensure that no resident doctor left work during duty hours. I vividly recall that once the father of a child came to the hospital at 2 am. He had no money for CSF investigation. Dr Khadwal had to ascertain what kind of meningitis the boy had. She offered money from her end. The stressed father rushed out only to come back without the report. He lamented that the lab was asking for extra charge of Rs 30/- for night service. Dr Khadwal instinctively turned to me asking if I had the money on me. 'I will return it to you tomorrow,' she told me. Of course, I was most willing to part with what I had. Later, when I saw the boy leave for home after a miraculous recovery I was grateful that a small contribution from my end had been of some worth. What is a better blessing in life than saving a dying child? There are countless accounts and instances of Dr Khadwal's dedication and kindness.

Later in my study and practice of clinical medicine, I found myself enjoying the inner psychological experience of dealing with medical problems. Doctors are often not taught about the human stories that lay beyond the study of human anatomy, physiology and biochemistry. It was in the course of my own practice that I realised that healthcare is fundamentally about social interactions. I would sit with my patients and ask them about the crucial moments and milestones in their life that meant the most to them. The sessions would last from five minutes to an hour and a half. Many patients needed gentle prodding or questioning and then they would talk, while I listened. My mind noted the conversations, and I found that these accounts painted rich portraits of struggle and hope. An offhand description of their illness, or, financial crisis would take on a deeper meaning.

Their conversations would reveal their resilience as also their hopelessness. The accounts would be both uplifting and distressing. A woman told me that she just found out that she had breast cancer. She had got hit in the chest by a cricket ball and was brought to the hospital where she ended up discovering that she was suffering from breast cancer. Another woman shared her tragic account of having been infected with HIV by her late husband. She could not re-marry, even though her new partner was ready to accept her. Her own guilt would not allow her to. A prisoner, who was also my patient, described how she had murdered her real brother-in-law. I was reminded of the heroism of people I had only need about in stories. I recalled a character in Shivani's story 'Chunali'. The heroism of a rickshaw puller reminded me of the character of Shambu Mahato in the film 'Do Beegha Zameen.' Real life would merge with reel and print life. I would get to know patients through their stories and it helped broaden my own horizons.

A doctor needs to learn the complete medical and social history of his/her patients. You have to probe, prod and nudge for information that brings you closer to a diagnosis. This helps to guide the patient in the right direction, empower the patient with the right attitude and give them hope and assurance. In my initial year as a resident doctor I would find myself devoting a lot of time listening to my patients. The clock behind me would keep ticking. I would often question myself. Why was I spending so much time getting to know a patient personally? I was only supposed to note the clinical case and go ahead with my job. During our daily rounds my team would be eager to move from one patient to another and.... I often had to come to terms with their impatience.

During my early years as a newly-qualified doctor I exhorted myself to read a lot of Hindi literary works by writers of eminence such as Dharamveer Bharati and Shivani. I also watched classic films and, in particular, the films of Bimal Roy, Satyajit Ray. I would romanticize my vocation. I found that in many of my patients and their cases rested the characters and situations I had read about in literature or seen on screen. This was a whole new world of maladies. To me, in fact, a few specific patients appeared to inhabit a higher plane of humanity.

As a doctor, I also read and assimilated the vast knowledge that medical science and, research offers. I combined it with my own gathered experience as a clinician. I believe that though diseases have a specific medical name, terminology and diagnosis that is to be applied uniformly to the patients suffering from the precise disease, still, every patient has to be treated differently. The disease can be common, but the body and the mind carrying it are different for individuals. Till date, I talk extensively to my patients. My practice is routine and yet not boring. Every patient is a unique person brimming with stories that offer me an insight into a vast array of thoughts, experiences.

I am a well-established orthopaedic surgeon today and my OPD is full. Day and night, I am in the company of patients suffering from disjointed joints, bone fractures, muscle pulls and spine disorders. Neglected trauma crowds my space. The patients are, on an average, not very literate and certainly not the best of communicators. Amid routinely hectic schedules, I consciously look for the brighter side of life in the case-stories of my patients. This desire has led to discovering little joys and humbling life lessons. Each case is a story of its own kind. I once read a sentence somewhere that has stayed with me. 'The universe is not made of atoms. It is made of tiny stories.' I remember smiling. My OPD tells me many stories. Some of the interactions turn out to be very rejuvenating.

One day, years ago, a 97-year-old Army veteran was rushed to my OPD with a fractured hip. He was a very determined nonagenarian on the way to being a centenarian. 'Doctor, just do my surgery. I do not fear death. I am ready for it anytime.' His family was apprehensive and reluctant that he go through with the procedure at his age. To me the man seemed physically and psychologically fit, with a strong urge to live. He was adept at fighting battles. I undertook the procedure and he lived for two more years after the procedure. What stays with me to-date are his war anecdotes and stories. He was a raconteur, an expert story-teller. He had fought World War II and had been summoned to train the Army in the Indo-China conflict of 1962.

I still recall his passionate assertion 'It was not the Chinese betrayal that defeated us Indians, but the failure of political leadership; Jawaharlal Nehru and Krishna Menon's arrogance. They believed that through diplomacy they would solve the crisis.' He also recalled having lived with Major Dhyan Chand, the legendary hockey player, in the Bagdogara base camp. He was bitter with the Indian government for having neglected him during his stay at the All India Institute of Medical Sciences (AIIMS). Upon his discharge from my treatment and care he had remarked, 'You are a good doctor, but I do not wish to visit you. I want to go to my final resting place. I do not fear death. I fear a life unlived. Death is not the enemy. It is suffering that is mankind's enemy. One should be alive in health and spirit till the end.'

TWINKLE is another case-story very dear to me. One day in the lobby of my OPD I saw a young, charming and smiling girl who was lying on a stretcher. I walked up to the her and to my shock found that both her lower limbs were very badly scarred. One of them was mauled and infected. Even more shocking was discovering that both her upper limbs had been amputated after a major accident. She had been electrocuted by a high tension wire while drying wet clothes on her rooftop. She had been rushed to Delhi's Safdarjung Hospital where her life did get saved, but her upper limbs had to be amputated. The worst befell her when she fell off a stretcher and broke her lower right limb that later got infected as well. She had to go through an arduous treatment and trial. A young girl of 25 had been handicapped for life. For me, as a doctor, the challenge went beyond just her physical rehabilitation. It was her mental and emotional well-being that needed attention.

In the course of her treatment Twinkle decided to reclaim her spirit. She treated her suffering as a challenge. She learnt to walk, live life and rehabilitate herself with the strength of her will and medical support. Twinkle, twinkled again with a sparkling smile. I too learnt a lesson. I realised that suffering is the only constant in human life and a handicap is just a state of mind. One can learn to be at peace with physical suffering through emotional strength and a pleasant countenance.

Sometime ago, on 16 August 2019, Twinkle sent me a lovely WhatsApp message—'Good Morning Sir, Twinkle here…so glad to inform you that I have been selected in AIIMS Rishikesh for a PhD in Yoga. I got a special gift in the AIIMS library…your fantastic book *In and Out of Theatres* …I can't explain how happy I was when I saw your name on the book…lovely experience. Thank you doctor.'

I messaged her back 'Wow Twinkle, I'm happy to see that you are doing so well!'

❧

TARA AUNTY is not just my prized patient case-story, but also represents a very dear part of my boyhood. In it lies the string of my first connect with Music and the Arts. My mother and Tara Aunty were once very dear friends. In Tara Sharma's musical wanderings and passion also lay the tragic text of her life. Before I go into that flashback let me confess that during my adulthood I had lost connect with Tara Aunty. Then one day, years later, that same Tara Aunty, our landlady from a distant past, was brought to my hospital as a sick and abandoned patient. She was brought to the hospital by a Muslim family who lived in a portion of her house. Sighting her in my medical environs, took me back to the August of 1979 when Tara Sharma came into our life in Bareilly and later came to be called Tara Aunty. She had shaped her own singing talent since the age of three and remained a most devoted student of the Rampur-Sahaswan Gharana of Hindustani classical music. Her great grandfather, Pandit Bimal Sharma, was considered the pioneer of harmonium playing in the Indian subcontinent. He was closely associated with Inayat Hussain Khan Saheb, the Indian classical vocalist and the founder of the Rampur-Sahaswan Gharana. It was in her company that I was exposed to the magic of classical and semi-classical music as a child. As a little boy, I would mimic *alaap* rendering. My first connect with music was also my first connect with the Arts. Tara Aunty wanted her three daughters of follow her musical passion, but circumstances denied her that wish. Even as a child, I could grasp that society, including my father, was very judgemental of Tara Aunty and her life choices. She had to depend on the patronage of the rich male members of the society for her survival. In my mother, Tara Aunty had found a very strong emotional and spiritual support. However, we shifted residences and lost touch with her.

Thirty years later, time stood still for a while, as I looked at Tara aunty. She wanted to hug me, but was physically unable to do so. She had fractured her hip-bone and was in excruciating pain. She had been bed-ridden for the past two weeks. I made an emotional promise silently, to my mother, that she would soon see Tara Aunty walk. My memory took me back to the moment when, for the first time in my life, I had heard the term 'raga'. It was also my first connect with 'Raag Desh' and Tara Aunty's rendition of it was beautiful. The lyrics were *'Taqdeer ka fasana jaakar kise sunayein/Iss dil mein jalrahi hai arman ki chitayen...'* It was from the 1963 film 'Sehra' and was rendered in two solo versions by Mohammad Rafi and Lata Mangeshkar, respectively.

What I regret the most is that moments before I could perform her surgery, Tara Aunty left the world on 2 November 2012. She did, of course, leave behind for me her 'fasana', her tale. The dead have no memory.

❧

I do ask myself often, 'How does one remain selfless and noble in today's consumerist and cut-throat world?' The answer is simple and yet not simple. We need to unclutter the mind and go back to the age of innocence, to more idealistic times when serving people was seen as the only salvation a doctor had to aspire to. Life passes us by as we rush to accumulate success, wealth and realize our ambitions. I'd prescribe that you take a pause, go find your own high school picture and look directly into the eyes of that young boy or girl. It can re- energise you and make you recall and draw the inspiration you need, to be greater than just your ambition.

Make it Happen

Tricolor wrapped around the shoulders
Crowds going wild, and I'll say I told you
Dreams too big, but enough to hold on to
I'll make it happen, watch me conquer.

When I entered the room, the boy lying on the operating table was sobbing, choking on his tears and almost convulsing.

'What happened young man? Does this not suit you? I wish you would keep calm and not focus on the pain.'

'Please doctor, could you please call my coach?' he pleaded.

'No.' My anesthetist said curtly.

The boy was sedated, so his mumbling gradually faded. His broken forearm was joined and plastered.

'How is my boy, doctor?' Someone grabbed my hand as I stepped out of the operation theatre.

'Oh, Patel? Yes, he is good. I think he will recover in six weeks' time.

'The boy is a national-level player. He belongs to the Army Boys' sports company,' The coach, Mr Singh, informed me.

'He can't play till he recovers, probably not for another three or four months,' I said.

'His career is at stake, he is our finest wrestler. Next month, he is supposed to play in Russia. He is one of the best we have, doctor. It wouldn't be an exaggeration to call him our future Olympian.'

'I'm so sorry but if it were up to me, every patient would go home in a day, but bones take time to heal.'

'Sir, your next patient is waiting for you,' my assistant informed me and I took my leave.

A few weeks later, Patel's plaster was removed, and he looked cheerful when he came to meet me.

'He barely slept last night in anticipation of getting back to the ring,' Mr Singh said.

'So, when can I start playing doctor?' Patel asked, looking rather restless.

'What would you like to hear?' I asked, playfully.

'That I can start playing from tomorrow. Well, can I?' Patel asked excitedly.

Not wanting to give him an affirmative answer before checking his arm thoroughly, I decided to change the topic.

'Which city do you belong to?'

'Kolhapur.'

'Oh, Maharashtra.' I said.

'What do your parents do?'

'My father is no more. He was in the Army and lost his

life in Kashmir. My mother lives in the village.'

'Why did you opt for wrestling?'

He smiled but didn't answer.

'When will I be back in the ring?' asked Patel again.

'Six more weeks, at least. You should refrain from any strenuous physical activity till then.' I cautioned him and his coach.

Both looked displeased.

'Sir, we came to you for a faster recovery,' Mr Singh said, rather rudely.

'Healing takes its natural time. The medicines will help for sure, but the right amount of rest is needed.' I said authoritatively.

I suddenly remembered that I shouldn't repeat a mistake that I had made in 2005, when MS Dhoni had come to us with Vivek Razdan. I had forgotten to click a picture with them at that time.

'Let's take a picture together with our future Olympian,' I said enthusiastically.

The boy's lips held a faint smile and his eyes twinkled.

It helped lighten the atmosphere in the room.

'You will definitely play for India in the Olympics,' I said with conviction.

'I just want to be back in the games for now doctor,' he said abashedly.

'Sky is the limit, my boy. People watch the Olympics because they want to believe in heroes.'

We clicked a picture and Patel left for his physiotherapy.

'Make it happen!' I said, whispering to the heavens.

The picture is ready and waiting to be framed, seeking its place on my personal wall of fame and I know in my heart that Patel will make it happen.

That Boy, Bhrungesh

Come judgement day
and the world pries pries
The lone wolf dies
But the pack survives.

'*B*hrungesh, the boy who never cried. The boy who won our hearts.'

Bhrungesh reached home, a village in Mysore. His family had lost all hope but the man defied the odds and survived. Notwithstanding his malady, there was nothing as pleasant as coming home again. Everything looked the same. Nothing had changed except for him.

For more than two weeks, he had been with us as a survivor of a train accident. To tell you the truth, at one point in the operating room I thought to myself, '*He should have died there and then. I couldn't have faced it if it was me. What will he do in his life. Will he be able to do theatre again? How will he manage his life from now on?*'

Three weeks ago he had been brought to my hospital in a semi-conscious state at around 11 p.m. I recognized him immediately as Bhrungesh, a theatre enthusiast just like me.

He had been travelling with a friend, Mahesh, from Haridwar to Benaras on a train. The general compartment was crammed with passengers. When the train was slowing down at the Bareilly station, Bhrungesh came near the door to get off but before he could even reach it, he was pushed out by the crowd. He slipped and fell through the gap between the train and the platform onto the tracks and was crushed under the train's wheels. Bhrungesh was taken to the civil hospital first, then to a private nursing home before he was brought to me.

He had significant injuries on his three limbs!

His Blood Pressure couldn't be recorded.

His skin was absolutely cold, carotid pulse was low and critical blood loss had landed him in hypovolemic shock: excess loss of blood that poses the threat of multiple organ failure. Besides fluid resuscitation, he required urgent blood transfusion.

There was no one to donate blood to him except his only friend Mahesh who was accompanying him. That night, I found myself dialing our ex hospital manager, Mr Kohli, who was actively involved in blood donation camps. He sorted it out.

Two workers, one cycle stand *wala* and a compounder were of O negative blood group. They donated their blood. The dressings of all three limbs were removed and I could not hold back my tears. Everyone in the operating room fell silent and only the chiming of the monitors could be heard.

I had never seen such macerated limbs. Both of Bhrungesh's upper limbs were almost amputated, being held together only by loose skin.

One of the lower limbs was mutilated too.

Meanwhile I got in touch with his family on the phone, sent photographs, explained his condition to them and took consent for the amputations. All this was beginning to get emotionally overwhelming but I had a job to finish and I couldn't let the situation get the better of me.

Finally, Bhrungesh was administered two units of blood and four units of fresh frozen plasma. A central line was inserted in his neck and guillotine amputation done for his upper limbs. The right lower limb was also badly damaged, but I couldn't get myself to amputate his third limb too. Anyhow, the thigh fracture was fixed, the crushed foot was held up with wires, with the hope that by some miracle the circulation from the preserved tissue would resume.

At around 5 a.m., Bhrungesh opened his eyes and asked for some water. He was stable now. However, the condition of the lower limb remained serious.

A day later, Bhrungesh was informed of another amputation but, surprisingly, he did not protest and underwent the surgery happily. His younger brother and some friends arrived to take care of him and he was shifted to a private ward.

Almost two weeks later, the Divisional Medical Officer (DMO) from the Northern Railway Office, Bareilly, came to meet me. He said that he wanted to know about Bhrungesh's condition, because he had to report it to the senior authorities.

I was happy that the Railways was finally taking an interest, even though it had been 17 days since the mishap. I was hopeful that the Railways would help him financially, and get him reimbursed under Railway's Accident Compensation Act or—taking his life- long disability into account—might even offer him some kind of a job. I was hopeful that they would help him to get back to Mysore for free. I updated the DMO about Bhrungesh's condition. The officer praised my work and even promised some monetary compensation for Bhrungesh. He also promised to send Bhrungesh to Mysore by train.

I was relieved and shared the good news with Bhrungesh and his friends. In the ward, his friends saw to his well-being personally, except for medication and dressings. Gradually they learnt these things too, and learnt them well. They were all theatre artists. They must have done bonding exercises with their group, like the one where they all hold hands and tie themselves into a human knot, and have to work as a team to free themselves.

That real human knot was visible to all of us, in private ward no. 102.

They took care of his back, regularly cleaning and massaging it twice a day. Every day, they took him to the washroom, washing and cleaning him with their own hands. I saw them feeding him, laughing and joking with him, keeping his spirits high.

Bhrungesh never cried over his injuries, on his circumstances, or even his disabilities. His smiles made them all smile! They did everything humanly possible to bring back normalcy to his mangled life.

Finally, Bhrungesh was discharged from hospital. All of them prayed for a safe journey back home. They met every staff member and thanked each one personally.

They carried him in their laps and laid him in a van that took them to the railway station. No person from the Railways ever turned up, not even to send him back home and he was never paid the compensation amount due to him. But Bhrungesh never complained. I was later told that he had started walking with the help of prosthetic legs and was teaching acting to young theatre enthusiasts.

Your win is never decided by the hand that has been dealt to you but by how you choose to play your cards, is what I always think about when I think of that boy, Bhrungesh.

No Place like Home

Where the children all play with dolls of clay,
Where the lemonade comes, served on an old tray,
Where humble smiles are thrown your way,
Where the mothers meet, over a pattern of crochet,
Let me brag, if I may,
Nothing compares to where I stay.

A long time after they had last been there, Mamta and her frail father-in-law visited my outpatient clinic.

'He is still living, despite his fair share of problems,' I thought, while greeting them as they entered.

'Stop moaning! You're in a safe place now,' said Mamta to her father-in-law, whom she called 'Baba'.

'For the last few days the pain in his joints has become more severe,' she said to me, looking very worried.

'Have there been any changes in his diet or lifestyle?' I asked Mamta.

'Not really, but it worsened after his gastric upset, which

flared up his joint pain. There must be new ways to treat arthritis and I am sure you know the latest and best treatment available. Kindly help him!' Mamta pleaded.

As I straightened myself, I noticed Baba's sunken eyes looking at Mamta, possibly searching for some kind of assurance that he wasn't going to die. She smiled at him in a comforting way.

'I have been taking care of him for more than two decades,' she added. I nodded. Mamta had been visiting my clinic for many years.

'Yes I know. It is nice to have people like you who take care of their family so selflessly.'

Mamta was married to Baba's only son when she was just 19. She came across as a quiet and elegant girl full of compassion. The marriage only lasted for three years before it ended due to her husband's illness, which led to his untimely death.

'We didn't have many years in our married life, but we had life in those three years and that was enough for me to stay back in the house where my husband, Aakash, was brought up and which held many memories for us,' Mamta told me.

'I was just 22 when Aakash passed away. There comes a time when you have to choose between turning the page and closing the book. I decided not to re-marry; I couldn't leave my in-laws alone. This place is my home, our home. But soon the childless house started to haunt all three of us,' she said.

'It just felt incomplete without children. We were looking for a someone to fill the void and emptiness left behind by Aakash.'

So, one day, I told my mother in law, 'I am not going to marry again, but you still have a good chance to give birth. You're just 40 years old, and Baba is not even 50, so why don't you try and have a child.'

'A year later, she gave birth to Anand. He changed our world. I didn't give birth to Anand, but he became the focal point of all our lives. As he grew, so did our hopes and dreams for him. One afternoon, Anand didn't return from school. He had an accident, and died on the spot, at the age of 15. Suddenly, in the blink of an eye, our lives were turned upside down once again. It took all our courage and strength to continue living after this tragedy,' she added, sadly.

'I couldn't give in to my grief as I still had aging in-laws who needed my help, now more than ever. I now spend my time looking after their needs and praying. Worldly affairs fail to interest me anymore. Since then, I've been visiting you with my in-laws. It's been more than ten years now. Even years of caring for them has not embittered me.

'You always give us hope. You are not just my doctor, but my confidante too,' she said gratefully.

'Thank you,' I said, touched. 'I remember, you told me once, that you had not consumed cereal for years, only fruits and dry fruit. Why did you do that?,' I asked Mamta.

'After Anand's death, I didn't eat cereal for years, as I was disappointed with life but now I have started eating them as I have yet again found a reason to live. I have adopted a girl, Anandi, who is six years old now. She has brought happiness and joy back in our lives,' she said with a smile.

'That's nice!' I said.

'Some people will leave you soon, but it's not the end of your story, it's just the end of their role. Our stories continue and it's our choice to make them happy ones or not.'

'Doctor, the night is the darkest just before dawn and I knew the dawn in my life was breaking, it had to.' Mamta looked poised as she strode towards her father-in-law, confidently, leading him out of my clinic and into the world she had painstakingly re-built for them, yet again.

Bittersweet

Sugar and candy,
And all its craze.
Sweet in a bite,
Once taken too much,
Becomes bitter to taste.
Lives lost many,
Such a plague.
Spoils the blood,
O what a waste!

'May I come in?' someone said, standing at my chamber entrance.

'Do you recognise me doctor?' asked my next patient.

'Yes, of course. I remember you, Kashish. How are you?'

Kashish looked leaner than the last time I had met her and the yellow saree she was wearing brought out the colour in her brown eyes.

'I'm good doctor, and I did lose a little weight in the past few years, isn't it good?' she replied enthusiastically.

'It's great!' I said, resonating her enthusiasm.

'My life has taken a new course. I got married and I now live in Benaras, a city famous for its mouthwatering delicacies. Since the wedding, on every weekend I used to eat something sweet and creamy until I got diagnosed with diabetes.'

That is really unfortunate for a person who loves to eat; I thought to myself.

'Though it was a huge shock, I was indifferent to the diagnosis as I didn't want to be petrified my entire life. It took me a lot of time and effort to adjust to the new situation. I have been able to lose weight and keep my habits under check, largely due to my husband and in-laws. They encouraged me to diet and exercise. In a way, diabetes has taught me self-discipline but, at the same time, I have a feeling of deprivation,' she said.

'Aren't you happy?' I asked her.

'Hmm…being a diabetic, I miss the guilty pleasures of life. Especially, when I see delicious food full of calories and carbohydrates all around me. Moreover, it doesn't feel good to be confined by specific rules,' Kashish said.

I usually begin my day with an authentic desire to keep myself healthy and fit. However, as the day progresses, this desire gets corrupted by the distorting voices in my head that tempt me to rebel. Living with this conflict 365 days a year is becoming too much and it is starting to affect my moods.'

Kashish sounded so pessimistic that I had to try and cheer her up. 'I would say, having diabetes does not mean you have to keep counting the calories or abstain from all delicious food. You must eat carefully, eat right and eat sensibly. Do not starve or deprive yourself, and definitely do not over-indulge,' I told her.

'What about my sweet tooth?' Kashish asked, hopeful, yet curious.

'There is no harm in indulging, if what you eat is within limits,' I reassured her.

'I just can't seem to stop myself when I see food,' she said with a chuckle.

'Then you already know the consequences of your actions,' I said.

'Oh doctor, you have confused me!'

'First of all, understand what is healthy and good for you. Remember, this is a process that takes time; you can't tackle everything at once. Make small changes in your habits, one by one, and things will slowly take a turn for the better.'

'I have developed some healthy habits doctor but I am struggling now,' she said, looking very disheartened.

'Let me tell you that diabetes is a rapidly progressive disease and India has become the 'diabetic capital' of the world. Some of our favorite celebrities are affected by it too. Sonam Kapoor and Fawad Khan are both diabetics even though they are health freaks,' I told her.

'Why are you naming celebrities, doctor?' She asked.

'I am naming them to make you understand that diseases don't discriminate between the rich or the poor, or between caste and religion. However, they can be managed with self-discipline, proper knowledge and correct guidance. With a positive attitude you can lead a normal, healthy and happy life,' I added.

'Certainly,' Kashish replied, looking more relaxed and hopeful now that her fears had been put to rest. Moderation is the key and a bittersweet truth behind managing lifestyle diseases.

101 Not Out

I may not have much left,
But Life is at what I'm adept
It made me a man, from a child
The Soldier on the field,
And the Lion in the wild.

Nawab Sher Khan underwent two hip surgeries in a period of 15 days at the age of 101.

He had been conferred with the title of 'Sher Khan' by the Governor of the then United Provinces (comprising Agra & Awadh), Sir Graham Haig, when the Nawab was in high school, because he had killed a lion.

The lion had accidentally fallen in a dug well and tried all sort of ways to climb out, but failed. Nawab saheb and his friends took advantage of the lion's helplessness and used a javelin, a sword and a spear, inflicting multiple wounds that made him bleed. The lion eventually succumbed to its wounds.

'There was nothing like wildlife conservation back then',

he smiled and told me. 'Rather, we were rewarded for killing the lion. Soon, it became apparent that Sir Haig and other British officers were interested in enlisting me in the British Indian Army to fight in World War II.

There were lots of posters doing the rounds (WW II).

'The British Indian army needs you for WWar II.'

They were offering the Indian soldiers a uniform, gun and money to fight in WWII. The Indian National Congress and our local leader Maulana Sheikh Waheed Ahmad Masood didn't like the fact that Indians were being dragged into WWII. Masood was the publisher and contributor to *Naqeeb*, a magazine for rebels, and I was the one who distributed it,' the Nawab said.

'In fact, the Quit India Movement was launched by Mahatma Gandhi to prevent Indian soldiers from fighting in World War II. Sheikh Masood Saheb welcomed Gandhiji on his arrival at Badaun, and led the procession on his horse while serving as a guide to Gandhiji through the streets and bazaars. Later that evening, Sheikh Masood's press was seized, but he managed to escape. Thereafter, Hasrat Mohani became his inspiration in mobilizing the youth to rebel against the British Raj', Nawab Sher Khan told me.

At the crack of dawn on 15th August 1947, the Nawab Sher Khan threw the British flag with his own hands and took pride in hoisting the tricolour. He was surprised that he still remembered all this and other memories of the years gone by.

'Perhaps the past beats inside me like a second heart', said the Nawab, one of the few people alive today to have witnessed the struggle and growth of our young nation.

Wish Upon a Star

While the night is young, and the moon grows large,
Over the city of flashing cars,
The sky is lit brighter, with two more stars.

'It's so late, already!' I complained to my anaesthetist. 'It's my fifth surgery in a row. We are soon starting the last one of the day', he replied and fell into his chair exhausted.

'Sir, there is a bleeding child in the emergency room. We have given him first aid, so could you please examine him now?' said a resident doctor suddenly rushing in.

Even though I was tired and had another surgery scheduled, I was reminded of Kailash Satyarthi's words where he said that 'every single minute matters, every single child matters, every single childhood matters.' I decided to postpone my surgery and reschedule it for the next day and went to see the child.

I found a four year old, pale and semiconscious, with a deformed and bleeding upper limb.

He needed blood, which was being arranged by the hospital staff.

For the next half an hour, I worked on fixing his multiple fractures. The bleeding had stopped and his condition was stable.

As I was heading home for the night a few people approached me to ask about the child,

'Sir, how is the child?'

'Are you all related to the boy? He needs someone to look after him in post-surgery.' I said.

'Sir his parents died on the spot, at the place of the accident. There is nobody accompanying him, we are just friends and neighbours,' they said.

'How did it happen?' I asked out of concern.

'Well that's an incredibly sad story doctor. During these days in Joshipura Majhola, there is a fair organised in honour of Basanti Devi. The child, whose name is Gaurav, and his family, live in Rudrapur. They attend the fair every year. Today was the last day of the fair and the family was enjoying a ride on the ferris wheel when one of the bars of their carriage came loose and the family fell out from high up in the air. Both his parents had injuries on the head and we couldn't even bring them to the hospital as they were already dead. We found Gaurav, at a distance, unconscious but breathing, and we rushed him here.'

The next morning, I saw a gaunt, old woman walking slowly towards me. She introduced herself as Gaurav's grandmother. She had adopted Gaurav's mother as a child. She did not have any other family. Gaurav was the only one left now.

His recovery was slow. He had a depressed fracture and we couldn't take any sort of risk as he was still semiconscious. In a week's time, Gaurav started responding to commands but was very quiet, as the trauma of the accident was still fresh.

As he opened his eyes and started to gain consciousness, he asked about his parents. He wanted to know which hospital they were in, and when he could go and see them. All visitors were asked the same question. His curious eyes and innocence made everyone's heart melt. He repeatedly said, 'My carriage had a loose bolt. I remember arguing with the man who was operating the ride to fix it but he ignored me and even baba didn't listen.'

Finally, after a few weeks, Gaurav was healthy enough to go back home with his grandmother.

He also found support in one of the neighbours and his fiancé who looked after him like their own son. After a month or so, Gaurav came for his follow-up visit. 'Uncle, do you know that my parents are also in this hospital?' he said.

I just smiled at him. He had not been informed of his parents' demise.

'Tell him! Suffering wounds us, but should not scar us for life', I tried to make his uncle understand. 'The sooner the better. Tell him right away!' I pleaded.

'Why don't you tell him doctor? Please, can't you do it?', his uncle requested.

I sighed and nodded, wondering how I was going to accomplish such a sensitive and grave task.

'Listen, Gaurav…when you reach home, go out and look at the sky; you will see your parents in the stars at night.

Call out to them and they will hear your voice. They will be looking down at you. They will be your companions when you are alone and frightened. Whenever you want to see them, you can find them among the millions of stars that twinkle in the sky and you will know it's them because two of them will shine the brightest for you.'

'Oh really?', Gaurav said happily. As he ran out of my chamber, he glanced up at the distant sky that was already growing darker with the promise of unveiling its countless treasures.

Something Borrowed, Something Blue

One of the seven, the shades of blue
The unknown, the mysterious, majestic and true
So special, yet born so few.
My clothes, your hair, those eyes and shoes
Take a look, and everything is blue.

'My hands are important too doctor, just like yours,' said the injured patient who was looking resplendent in a blue outfit.

'Of course,' I smiled. I started looking at her X-rays. She had broken both the bones in her forearms.

'So, how did it happen?' I asked.

'It was a trivial fall from a table, I lost my balance. God has given us two hands to clap and entertain to earn our bread,' she said candidly.

Oh! She was a trans-woman (hijra), I realized. Now I could understand the context of what she was saying.

Rukhsar was well versed in English, Hindi, Urdu and

Telugu. She was home till her parents were alive in Hyderabad. She went to Kendriya Vidyalaya Jr. College, Golkonda School and later she studied at Andhra Christian Theological College.

'The thing about trans people is, we feel very normal, it's the way we are. Only when people don't treat us like everyone else do we feel otherwise,' Rukhsar said sadly.

'Until I was about 13, I didn't know I wasn't a girl. School and college was an extremely difficult period since I got bullied a lot. I was picked on for being different. Everyone mocked my sexuality.'

'I used to live in Dubai with my brother and worked as a receptionist in one of the hotels, but I left and came back to Hyderabad because my brother's social life was starting to suffer because of me. My relatives didn't like my occasional visits to my own house. They feared that I would claim my share of the property,' Rukhsar said bitterly.

'This life has shown me some of the worst and best that humanity has to offer and I have finally become part of a community that has accepted me and loves me the way I am. As for my part, they are my family now and I love them.'

Our only expectation from life is happiness and respect, I thought to myself.

The colour blue spiritually signifies the healing power of God (in the Bible), which the *hijras* wish upon the families of those who welcome them graciously. It represents biblically, the word of God.

Also, blue is the colour of the sky and sea. It is often associated with depth and stability. It symbolises trust, loyalty, wisdom, confidence, intelligence, faith, truth, and heaven.

Blue is considered beneficial to the mind and body. It slows down human metabolism and produces a calming effect. Blue is strongly associated with tranquility and calmness.

'*Everything turned blue,*
I finally found peace in everything.
I'm no longer afraid.
And the calmness in me
Shines through my eyes.
May the power of blue always be with you.

No Strings Attached

A dance of fate, is all it takes
One to jive, one to break.
Strings aligned, for all but one
Cruel it may seem, fascinating to some
That marionettes, they are made for fun.

'Boy, you look so grown up!' I exclaimed in wonder, watching one of the most challenging patients I had ever worked upon. And he was a sight to behold.

After years, the father-son duo was in my cabin again.

'Do you remember his name Doctor?' the father asked.

'How can I forget you both?' I replied. The man's face broke into a grin.

'It makes me so happy to remember the day we met doctor, the day Durgesh was born and I was asked by the obstetrician, 'Do you really want to keep this child? He is arthrogrypotic.' '

Arthrogryposis Multiplex Congenita (AMC), is a lifelong

disability which would haunt the infant. All his joints were going to be curved and hooked for life.

'The doctor's question bewildered me for a few seconds. How could I give up on my child? Disabled or not, he was mine to look after. I took a deep tremulous breath and asked the obstetrician, 'What course of treatment can we pursue?'

'You can see an orthopedic doctor,' the obstetrician suggested.

Though deeply troubled, I was instantly determined to see an orthopedic doctor. After meeting you, I was a bit relieved. You told me that the only hope of getting his joints straightened out depended on immense patience and hard work we both had to put in.'

'Do you remember? Do you remember Durgesh?'

'Yes, I do remember most of it, not so vividly his initial days, but I do recall his countless plasters and numerous surgeries.'

'Seventeen plasters and six surgeries,' his father replied. Durgesh's father's emotive narration broadly brought back my memories of Durgesh's treatment.

'My gosh, what a challenge!' was my first reaction on seeing Durgesh.

Thinking about it now, how did I even accept it? It was one of those cases that helped me in establishing myself as a sincere practitioner.

Before committing to Durgesh I had the clear advantage of surgically working on more than 100 cases of club foot during my Masters degree, my thesis being 'Correction of club foot deformities'.

Though I had no experience of curing children with AMC, I knew that it was kind of an extended version of the 'club foot' that usually involves all four limbs.

During the course of treatment, Durgesh and I both faced a lot of difficulties and uncertainties. I did not know while operating on him whether that would be his last surgery or would he need more.

I had to apply the fixator several times, sometimes the pin would get infected or become loose and I had to remove it before reinstating it. After the surgeries the regular dressings and plasters seemed never-ending. Sometimes, I felt overwhelmed and other times his father seemed frustrated on account of the endless treatment.

'Leave it doctor, let nature take its course,' the father would say miserably.

'I am not even charging any fees, don't lose hope so soon. Have some patience. He is much better than the day he was born. Don't you notice the difference in the shape of his limbs? Isn't he improving?'

Discussions, explanations, assurances and differences were an integral part of the treatment. Durgesh was improving but the recovery was slow. It was taking a toll on both father and son.

At six years of age, his condition improved greatly and Durgesh starting walking with braces and support. He started eating by himself, and even went to school for the first time. Following this, they did not come for regular check-ups but his father kept me apprised of Durgesh's progress.

At the time we met again he was studying in the 9th

standard and was managing the sales counter in their family restaurant.

His father said to me, 'I wish he was walking without braces, he has been my lucky charm. Despite the struggles I have never looked back in my life. I'm thankful for what we have achieved so far, but I'd rather see him recover fully and walk straight, without any support.'

'He can easily manage to lead an independent life.' I said reassuringly.

'Throw your braces, let's see how you walk,' I ordered Durgesh.

'Can I take a stick?' he asked.

'No.'

'I will fall...'

'No, you will not, give it a try!'

Durgesh removed his brace hesitantly and started hobbling, yet he managed to walk some distance without any support. I noted the remedial measures that had to be taken to improve his walk.

'I was very sure Doctor, that you were going to deliver on your promise one day. I often cried watching him struggle. They were tears of pain and worry for my only son, but today my tears are of relief and joy.' Durgesh's father murmured.

Father and son went home happily. Perseverance and hard work had contributed to their success.

Some days later, a child suffering from the same condition was brought to me and it reminded me of the words of Mark Twain— 'No occurrence is sole and solitary but is merely a repetition of a thing which has happened before and perhaps often.'

'I don't have the courage and patience to treat such patients any more and I can't promise anything,' I told the parents.

'You come and see me again when she is a month old'.

'Let's see what happens, I will decide then.'

As they left, I saw a glimmer of hope in their eyes and I already knew that she was going to be my next AMC patient.

Maybe I do have the patience and courage after all.

Boon or Bane

Pleasure and pain, come hand in hand
It's hard to tell a Hero, from a Villain
In a foreign land
Motives can be wrong, or simply out of warmth
But never judge a man, who saved a life
Who hurt himself, while plucking your thorn.

'Stop!' I ordered my driver to turn around and go back at once.

I cancelled my plan of attending a family function and went back to the hospital.

The operating room which I had left an hour ago was not as busy as it appeared now.

Mrs D'Souza was still intubated, surrounded by technicians, chiming monitors and worried doctors, who were sparing no effort to revive her.

I gazed at the monitor through the door.

'She had seizures just now,' one of the doctors whispered.

Once again, I gazed down at the reduced heart rate on the monitor, not responding to repeated medication.

'She has disturbed autonomic regulation Sir.' It was the voice was of a physician who had just entered the room, and my gaze shifted to him.

The anesthetist briefed him about the surgery and how she was not responding to reversal or to pain. Even after plenty of fluids, her urine output was negligible.

'Then give her more fluids,' the physician instructed.

'I have already given enough, she might develop congestive failure.' The anesthetist feared further complications.

'No sir, half a litre will be fine, her pressure is still on the lower side,' he said.

My eyes were fixed on the urine catheter. I twisted her catheter tube several times to see if there were any drops coming from the bladder, but nothing.

Once again, fear gripped me. Somehow, I gathered the courage to have a few words with Mrs D'Souza's family to brief them about the unfortunate turn of events.

At that moment, she was still deeply comatose, though her blood pressure had stabilized.

Suddenly, a drop of urine dripped down in the urometer and my eyes widened. Another good response!

In a trice, few more drops were visible. 'Hey look at that,' I exclaimed in disbelief, as her condition started to show improvement.

Finally, Mrs D'Souza was shifted to the ICU, and her son was allowed inside.

It took a while to secure her tubes, but her pressure went

down again and she needed vasopressors. Her condition seemed unstable and she was in a precarious situation even after eight hours of surgery.

I had to focus on the other patients waiting their turn, so I casually walked over to the operating room, joined by my new anesthetist, carried out a few operations, and cancelled the rest of my appointments for the day.

Before leaving, I wanted to check on Mrs D'Souza in the ICU. I glanced at the clock. It was 4 a.m.

With a pounding heart, I looked through the ICU window.

'Gosh! Is she conscious?' I said rather loudly.

'She just regained consciousness,' one of the technicians told me.

She was biting the tube and struggling to get rid of it, but her limbs were fastened to the bed.

When I looked at the intensivist, he was all smiles.

'Could you please extubate her?' I requested.

'Sure sir, I was just waiting for you to come.'

'Great!'

I met the family and brought them with me to see her.

Mrs D'Souza was fully awake, but her speech was slurred.

'What has happened to me? I had come for treatment, but it feels like someone has put me in a jail. They have placed such heavy shackles on me, can't you see doctor? I want to be home for my grandson's wedding.'

I am being punished for no reason, and you're enjoying it! Just wait, God will punish you,' she said admonishingly, as she turned to me.

'Believe me, I'm already being punished, Aunty.' I smiled at her and left, relieved.

Even doctors go through the same fears as a patient's family. We feel responsible for our patients and are fearful of things going wrong.

The parking lot was lit by the faint yellow light of the breaking dawn, when I came out of my hospital.

I opened the car door and stumbled onto the seat to catch a few winks.

I opened the window and a sudden gust of wind ruffled my hair.

I couldn't help but fold my hands in prayer, thankful that the operation had been a success.

Dare to Dream

All I want,
What everyone wants,
Is for dreams to come true
Not nightmares, that still haunt.

'Whenever there is an overcast sky, my joints hurt me.' Once very agile and sure-footed, 75-year-old Vir Singh limped to the chair opposite me.

'Doctor, these joints are troubling him more than he admits,' said his daughter who was accompanying him.

Why doesn't he admit that he is in pain? I wondered.

'It's only the weather that affects me doctor, otherwise I'm fine,' he said.

'It's osteoarthritis,' I told him.

I explained how a change in atmospheric pressure stimulates the pain in degenerative joints.

'I have always been very active and well-disciplined in my life, like my father who was a Hawaldar in the Fourth

Kumaon Regiment. I always walked briskly just like him. I was a teacher in Government Inter College (Pithoragarh). Besides walking to school every day, I would walk to Kali Landing, an old tumbledown lumber-wharf on the Kali River used by the Army to train soldiers. It was usual for us to walk five to ten miles a day.'

He couldn't understand the reason for his arthritis.

'Now everyone has their own vehicle.

'The "good old days" were not as comfortable as today, but certainly more idyllic, active and healthy. Terms like local and organic, hormone free, 'gluten free', pesticides free and Artificial didn't exist,' he said with a sigh.

'In our childhood, pulses like Gehet and Bhatt used to prevent so many diseases. Burash, maduwa, aloe, asparagus were wonder herbs of our times.

Even our village astrologers were masters of their science. They could predict the exact day of rain almost a month, in advance and they were not as greedy as today's so-called astrologers.

The whole world has become so different, doctor, everything has changed; the climate, the mountains; and most of all—people.

Even my brother, whom I helped educate, went to Singapore to pursue science, never to return home, not even once. I bear no grudges, we still write to each other and talk on the phone. Well, he has his own reasons,' Vir Singh said.

He had so much contempt towards the world, it was hard to believe that he didn't resent his brother.

'Why didn't you join the Army like your father? Were

you not inspired by him?' I asked.

'Of course, I was inspired. I wouldn't have made seven attempts if I wasn't. I passed each physical test,' he said proudly.

'Why didn't you join the Army then?' I asked, surprised.

'Oh! This is going to make you laugh. I failed each time because of my abnormal dental condition.'

'What?'

'I only have 20 teeth.'

He snapped open his jaw to show me. He started laughing at himself, but the laugh echoed sadness and unfulfilled desires.

'Life is not about living in the past doctor, don't pity me. Life is about accepting the things that cannot be changed and making the best of what you have', he said resolutely.

As I write about him today, I am haunted by a question: how many of us are privileged enough to live our dreams and how many of us can only dare to dream?

God's Plan

Riches or wealth, and beauty melts
The cars you wash, instead of yourselves
The houses you paint, or your cooped up tent
In the end what counts
Is the mark you leave, if you made a dent.

'What's the point of living to a ripe old age, if you can't enjoy yourself?'

The granny arrived mumbling. The old woman made herself comfortable in the chair opposite me.

'Doctor, her name is Zanki Devi. She's my mother and she's ninety three years old.' said Rahul, her son.

'No she's ninety five,' corrected Suhani, Rahul's wife and Zanki Devi's daughter-in-law.

'She has never visited any specialist in her life, doctor. She's the healthiest and strongest woman I've ever seen. She wouldn't be here today, if not for this terrible pain.'

Rahul then went on to describe her pain to me, and while

I was examining his mother, he continued talking.

'She has, alas, become the helpless person she always feared of becoming, so we convinced her to visit you. Earlier in her life, she always treated her ailments with herbs that she used to keep in store. She has always been her own boss. She lived at our ancestral house in Dewalthal, Pithoragarh, looking after everything on her own. She loved working in the fields, milking cows and looking after the cattle.'

I could guess from the way he was speaking about his mother, that she was a strong and independent lady.

'She has been living with us since she left Dewalthal, a few months after my father's death.'

'She never visits any relatives, not even her own daughter. She only loves me,' her daughter-in-law said proudly.

Zanki Devi felt better after her epidural shot, and started talking to me.

'I have always been religious, doctor. I am a Mahadev devotee, he is always with me. If you believe in him, you'll see Mahadev open new doors for you, just like how I was brought to see you. Through the many struggles in my life, my faith has been the only thing I have held on to. No matter what, I never question God's plan for me. Old age never ends, but it brings you to your ultimate rest. I have seen all and done all and I have no regrets. You are still young, doctor, and have a lot to experience. I hope you never lose your smile and enthusiasm,' she said.

It's very rare to meet a person who is that satisfied with their life and has little to complain about. Zanki Devi was one of them. She reminded me of my youth and the many things I had yet to accomplish in my life. After she left I was reminded of the words of Robert Frost—*And miles to go before I sleep. And miles to go before I sleep.*

Priceless

O Granny of the stall,
Would you tell me what you've got?
Some veggies, fruits and some nuts,
All handpicked, fresh from the shrubs!
How much do I pay for this stuff?
'Don't worry,' said the Granny
'I got you, little cherub!'

Whenever Ladla's mother entered my cabin, I easily recognised her by the sounds of her cane thumping on the floor.

She always bypassed the crowd and directly entered my chamber. She had the privilege of seeing me, whenever she wanted. She had a long history with the hospital and me.

It was almost a decade ago, when I first met her as the mother of one of my trauma patients, Ladla. She had always been outspoken, and a tad overbearing at times, but never boring. She had become far too familiar with me and treated me like her son. Her ailments, aches and pains kept us in regular touch.

Over the years, she had to undergo two surgeries in a row: one for her spine and another one for her knee. Her usual visits were never accompanied by an outpatient slip. Moreover, she always brought along some edibles with her, like peanuts, roasted grams, fresh vegetables or seasonal fruits.

Her visits were always accompanied by a fresh stream of family stories.

'Like most people, I have also had my ups and downs; more downs than ups though. I had hoped that Ladla will be my support in the twilight of my life, but I was wrong. My future holds nothing.'

She always shared with me the stories of how she earned her livelihood. Selling vegetables and peanuts somehow ensured her survival.

'You are the only person whom I believe in now. This is for you, it's fresh, just take it home,' she would say. Her gestures and language reflected her compassion.

Sometimes she would wait for me, till I had seen my last patient; and was free from the day's work, often till the last minute of my office work was complete.

One day, she came to my cabin bypassing several patients as usual. I got a little disturbed by her arrival as she seemed very agitated and angry.

'I lost my bag in the tempo, do you think the driver will come back and return it to me?' she grumbled.

'What did you say?' I asked with a frown. I was busy reading a report.

She paused, smiling at her own impetuosity.

'It was a bag of peanuts that I bought for you for ₹60. How could I visit you empty handed, tell me?'

'I don't know how I forgot to pick up the bag while I was getting off! It is the first time I bought something as there was nothing in my house which I could bring for you.' With every sentence she sounded more disappointed.

She sounded like she had lost something very expensive. *Such simplicity*; I thought. It was not only her affection but her energy and love that touched me.

After all these years, I still remember her with a lot of warmth and love. The gift of the peanuts was just ₹60 but the thought behind it was priceless.

All About Time

Once it was yours,
Now it is mine,
Designed by nature
There's a fine line
Between getting played
Or playing with time.

It must have been around 1 a.m., I was surprised to see my doctor friend in the Emergency Room.

'Hey Sanjeev, all well?' I asked.

'Yeah, I just came to visit an emergency patient on my friend's request. Some guy from Mumbai who met with an accident. His name is Alam,' he said, stifling a yawn.

'Oh! We have that man sedated as he has a damaged arm. The X-ray reports don't look very good and we will have to operate on him.' I explained briefly to my friend.

He thanked me and got on his phone to inform the patient's family and departed soon after.

Now my gaze fell on Alam lying on the bed looking at me with a dazed expression.

I greeted him with my normal curtness, 'I'm waiting for the rest of your reports to come and I will get back to you as soon as I receive them.'

'No sir, please don't go. Tell me what has happened to me?' Alam looked evidently anxious.

'Your arm was crushed in an accident but don't worry, we're planning to operate on it soon to minimise the damage.' I said calmly.

'Will I be able to get back to my job?' he asked.

'What do you do?' I asked.

'I am a realtor. It's my own venture. We've only just started and the formal inauguration is due. My presence is mandatory in the office.' Concern was clearly etched on his forehead.

'You can get back to your job easily in a few days' time. You'll need some help though, as you can't drive on your own,' I informed him.

'How much time are we talking about, doctor?' he asked impatiently.

I calmed him down, and slowly explained the steps of the treatment and all the phases of recovery while answering all his questions simultaneously.

'How much time before I can ride my bike?' he sounded frantic now.

'How much time till I am able to sign documents? How long will it take for my fractures to heal? What will you do for my damaged nerves? Can you please tell me whether I will recover completely?' He threw a volley of questions at me, one after the other.

'I'd be lying if I said your hand will be perfect by tomorrow. It will take time but you will recover completely. So, put all your fears to rest,' I said reassuringly.

A day later, we met and shook hands, his arm hanging loose at the wrist. His dressings were done and his condition seemed satisfactory overall. A few people from Dargah Ala Hazrat visited him who were acquainted with me as well. Alam was well enough to travel and was advised to get his tickets booked for Mumbai.

'So, you will be discharged the day after,' I said cheerfully. 'You must be happy, aren't you?'

'Sir, I want to talk to you alone if you have got some time,' his face had lost all its light.

So, my team of junior doctors and nursing staff stepped out, leaving me alone with Alam in his room.

'I'll get straight to the point, sir. Just hear me out!' a nervous Alam mumbled.

'A few years ago, due to demonetisation my real estate business suffered great losses. The sector faced a big slump. I lost a lot of money so I decided to start something new.'

He continued, 'On the eve of Eid, I shifted my office to Kalyan. This new venture had stressed my already dwindling finances, but I hoped that things would improve.

It was my father's wish that I pay a visit to Dargah Ala Hazrat in Bareilly and Ajmer Sharif, before I start my new venture. If this accident hadn't happened, I would be in Mumbai now.' He sighed heavily.

'In the past four years I've hit rock bottom. I couldn't even claim my health insurance, as it expired just before Eid. So I'm no longer covered. I was a health insurance agent for years and forgot to renew my own policy. Unbelievable, isn't it?'

Alam's throat constricted and his eyes welled up.

I could understand his distress. He worked for medical insurance, yet didn't have a policy for himself when he needed it the most.

The next day, Alam was getting discharged and he looked happy.

'I can't thank you enough doctor!' he said on seeing me.

'For what?'

'For…getting me off the hook!'

'Oh, it's all right.'

'I mean it sir,' he said with gratitude.

I nodded, smiled courteously and left his room.

It is ironic that sometimes the things we do for others we take granted for ourselves. Like Alam, who helped many people cover their medical expenses but could not pay for his own. Doctors these days are dealing with Covid-19, the biggest pandemic the world has ever seen and many of them have helped save numerous lives but succumbed to the virus themselves.

The smallest of gestures can sometimes make all the difference.

Like a Butterfly

So far away, yet so close
A butterfly, in a world of its own;
Neither too up, nor too down
Its territory, is the middle ground;
Hard to touch, harder to catch
A world of its own, in a world lost and found.

Sometime ago, her time was tough in the hospital, but she dared to be tougher.

Her illness seemed to beat her, but she dared to fight back.

Divya is not a regular a nine-year-old girl.

She was in the hospital for 23 days, with a copious discharge from her back, fighting with dreaded anaemia and septicaemia. Even when everything seemed to fail, she would smile from behind her oxygen mask.

Today, she entered, with the same smile on her face, it's her trademark. She seemed so genuinely sweet, with a hint of shyness.

'She wants to go to school since it's been three months now, sir!' her mother said.

'Alright, but no school bag! Your back is not strong yet,' I said patting her gently.

'Imagine going to school without a bag?'

She twirled and it reminded me of a butterfly swaying in the wind, her spirit shines on.

On seeing her smile again an unexpected warmth rushed through me. Sometimes, simple and innocent grit can be more inspiring than anything else.

Poison Ivy

Some are dull, others too brave
A combination of two, digs his own grave.

'Oh, you look better today.'

'Yes, I am!' replied Ali.

'Are you my doctor?'

'No, your doctor is the plastic surgeon who deals with cases related to burns.'

'But I have never seen him.'

'Yes, maybe because your eyes were so swollen. You were in a really bad shape.' I told him.

'Well, I'm glad you have come out of a serious condition, even though burns seldom heal so fast. By the way, I am rather curious to know how you burnt yourself?' I asked.

'I had seen boys blowing fire from their mouths and that always excited me,'

Oh no! I knew where this was going.

He continued, 'The day of my uncle's wedding, we all

sneaked into the parking lot, and stole petrol from a bike. From what I had seen before, I just had to hold the fire up and blow out. But when I tried, I couldn't do it and inhaled the petrol instead. My face caught fire!'

'Oh, so you had never done it before?' I had to confirm.

'No, I had just seen a few boys from our village doing it but let's not talk about it. Tell me what I can eat, instead. Chicken?' he asked, changing the topic.

'Of course, you can eat chicken.'

'Banana, can I eat a banana?'

'Why not? You can eat anything you want, anything!' I assured him.

'I'm in the hospital and my parents don't allow me to eat fried food.'

'Who says you can't eat fried things? You are not sick. You just burned yourself and you are a lot better now, so you can eat anything.'

'Really? I hope you aren't joking or making fun of me. I will ask my doctor also,' he said.

'As you wish,' I shrugged my shoulders and smiled.

'But I hope you will not try this stupid thing again.'

'Yes I won't, certainly not with petrol. I made a mistake. This time, I'll use kerosene instead.' Ali said confidently.

All I could do was stand there with my mouth open.

Reminiscence

Ties break
and people fall apart
Nothing is as it seems
Till fate plays its card.

Rahmat Bhai got himself treated for his recurring shoulder dislocation after suffering from 25 years of pain and disability.

He hesitantly came into my chamber and introduced himself, 'I am from your ancestral village doctor; it's 500 kilometres from here. Your mother knows me.'

Two days later, when I was telling my mother how successful the surgery had proven to be for Rahmat Bhai, she reminisced how his father had been so well acquainted with my grandfather. Those were the days of *'zamindari'*.

She recalled how Rahmat Bhai sang beautifully on his kettledrums for more than a week, to celebrate my birth.

'Your grandfather joyously donated a piece of land to

Rahmat's father,' mother said.

A few years ago, I came to know how Rahmat's happy family life had turned upside down when his wife was diagnosed with malignancy and his elder son met with a fatal accident.

Both his loved ones perished in their struggle, leaving him only with a son, who later settled in Dubai and is now looking after his father.

The people who were once connected with my family, whom I didn't even know of till now, had suffered such a great ordeal at the hands of fate. I sympathised deeply.

It was also fate that years later I would repay him for singing at my birth, by treating him.

Although I hoped, I could have met him at a better time in his life.

Unordinary

Out of those who waste away
One stands out
Truly unordinary
The underdog, among the depraved.

That evening, Shivank's parents were standing in the Emergency room, when I entered to see him for the first time. The uncertainty surrounding his condition was visible in their eyes.

'Oh no!' I whispered in a choked voice.

I could see the fatigue on Shivank's face, but there wasn't any fright in his eyes.

I gave him a thumbs up and smiled at his bravery.

Shivank was sent to the operating room to be examined by the plastic surgeon. It was crucial because the preservation of his limb now rested in the hands of the surgeon.

We were in the OR together, when we got chatting, 'I applaud your courage, Shivank.

You know, you have a very good name. Who gave it to you?' I asked.

'I don't know,' he replied.

'So tell me, how did this happen?' I asked.

'This evening, when I got home, my mother reminded me of the fodder that I had forgotten to bring from the mill. It is my duty to feed and water the cattle. The mill was going to close soon so I rushed to get some. As I lifted the bag, I found it heavier than expected.

'Uncle, could you please help me keep the bag on my bicycle?' I asked the shopkeeper, but he ignored my request and rudely waved me away,' Shivank said casually.

'So I tried to lift the heavy bag myself. However, a few threads from the bag suddenly got caught in the wheels of the machine and in the blink of an eye, my hand and clothing became entangled in the drive shaft of the grist mill.

When the machine was switched off, my hand was barely hanging by the skin, and there was blood all over. The mill owner just left me stranded there and ran away.'

'How could he do such a thing to a small boy?' I was furious.

'My father was not home, so my mother was informed and I was brought to the hospital.'

Shivank had to undergo four surgeries in a span of 20 days to save his arm. I never once heard him complain or cry during his stay.

The condition of his limb improved gradually. The shape looked good and the limb was functioning reasonably well at the time of his discharge.

The mill owner never once visited the hospital or helped Shivank monetarily.

A few days later when Shivank came for a check-up I enquired about his studies. 'Your studies must have been adversely affected because of the mishap?.'

'No they haven't. I am very regular with my academic work,' Shivank replied brightly.

'Oh, going to school with this plaster bandage, I see.'

'Yes, I took my exams as well.' Shivank proudly informed me.

'How did you write them, did you take a writer?' I asked.

'No I wrote all of them myself.'

'How?'

'I am left-handed, sir.'

'That is fantastic Shivank!' I chuckled.

Sometimes even tragedy comes with a saving grace.

The Little Man

A face so keen, eyes so sharp
No hesitation, not for a moment
Face so little, but it sees all
What a little man! What an ill fall!

I was on my regular rounds when I noticed a child standing all by himself, confidently, with one arm stretched towards the attendant.

'Iqrar Bhai, can you please insert my intravenous catheter? My brother couldn't come today.'

I was observing him with an amused expression. He was not scared like most children when they see a needle, his arm didn't tremble and he didn't cringe or turn his face away when the needle was inserted.

I strode towards him.

'Hi there! What's your name?' I asked.

'Pakodi.'

'What?' I burst out laughing.

'Yes sir, he is Pakodi and his twin is Samosa,' the attendant replied with a chuckle. 'They are crazy about snacks, and so we named them accordingly. They have been coming here since they were born as they were diagnosed with Thalassemia Major.'

'The hospital is like a second home for us,' Pakodi promptly responded.

'Have you come here alone?' I asked with a smile.

'My brother usually accompanies me, so that we get the blood transfusion on the same day but he couldn't come today. My parents are working, so they can never come with us.'

'How often do you come for transfusions?' I asked.

'It depends. Sometimes it takes two transfusions, and other times we have to come three times a month,' he said.

'Don't you feel scared, coming alone?'

'Why?' he asked with a bewildered expression.

'Fearful, that something could go wrong…' I said.

'Worse than my illness? I don't think so,' he said, matter-of-factly.

Suddenly, the thought of his illness sent a shiver down my spine and I became quiet.

I took him in my lap and ruffled his hair. So little yet so mature.

'My dear, can I have the honour of getting a picture clicked with you?'

He smiled and nodded.

His treatment was over and he walked out the door with his head held high. To live and fight another day.

Euphoria

A bottle of wine, little sorrow of mine
The wind picks up, I holler into the night
My shadow looks strange, I wonder why
Is it a dog, or is it just the wine
Or is it simply my beautiful mind.
A chilling sensation creeps up my spine
And I double up to the side with a whine
My mind goes blank, pupils blown wide
Cold sweat, euphoric smile
At the same time, is truly divine.

'Why don't you just stop his treatment doctor? You've got more needy patients than him. I doubt if he will ever improve, he has always been wayward since his father died.' Mrs Bajaj grumbled, complaining about her son.

After an awkward silence, her son glanced at me with a mischievous smile and said, 'From now onwards, I will listen to you and mother, and I promise to behave.'

'Do yourself a favour and stand by what you say. Your mother is not supposed to take care of you, yet she does! Don't you know how much effort she has put into your treatment?' I admonished him.

'Yes doctor, make him promise that he will quit tobacco and smoking,' Mrs Bajaj intervened. 'I have struggled my whole life to make ends meet and raise him and never thought he would turn out to be so irresponsible.'

'I forgot to tell you earlier, that he drinks as well. On the day of the accident, he had consumed alcohol. Though he knows his father died an alcoholic, he still doesn't hesitate to drink.'

Mrs Bajaj said with displeasure.

'Promise your mother that you will give up smoking and drinking,' I said, sternly to the boy.

'Forget it doctor, he will swear on my life in front of you now, but forget his promises the next day. I know him,' said the mother.

'Never mind doctor, my mother is always complaining about me. Whatever I do, it won't change her attitude towards me.'

As the boy and his mother walked out, I knew that his promise, like her heart, was going to be broken.

The Hero Lies in You

Batman has Robin, Spiderman's got Gwen
If you count me in, I'll be a perfect Ten.
Superman has a cape and Ironman, his suit
I'll save the World, as a Hero recruit.
I won't fly or punch the bad guy
Just be the good man, my momma described.
Kind and fair to all his tribe
And most of all, be the one who never lied.

'Doctor saheb, we are in your city to perform, just like we promised,' Susheel ji made me realise that it was the 30th of July.

'Hope the arrangements are to your liking? 'I asked.

'Oh yes, we have settled down comfortably. Thank you, very much.'

'Doctor, just wanted to ask you something about my son, Abhay.' Susheel ji sounded hesitant. 'You know he plays the protagonist in this play, right? Well he's a little unwell today.

He has had cough and fever since morning and he has to perform in the evening. Could you please suggest something so he feels better?'

'Yes, sure. I'm sending someone with the medicines right now and I'm looking forward to your performance. All the best!'

I was really looking forward to watch the play 'Bade Bhai Saheb', written by Munshi Prem Chand, that was being performed by the Rang Visharad Theatre Club from New Delhi.

Interestingly, the father and son duo were playing the main characters, Bade Bhai and Chote Bhai, respectively; Abhay was only 12 years old.

As I stepped into the theatre, I noticed that it was full to its capacity and the audience was silently waiting for the most sought-after performance of the festival.

The play began with a lot of expectations and everything seemed to be going smoothly. Nevertheless, I could feel that something was amiss. The audience couldn't tell but I noticed how Abhay and other characters were hiding his coughing in between dialogues, through fine improvisations on the stage. Abhay seemed short of breath while delivering his dialogues even though he was throwing all his energy into the character.

Abhay's parents were also on the stage helping him constantly. His mother was playing his friend. She was holding cough syrup in her hands and putting it in his mouth at every chance she got. Abhay was holding a bottle of warm water as well, taking small sips throughout.

He was trying his best to live the character amid the chaos, without letting the audience know. A few of us, including the District Magistrate of Bareilly, knew about Abhay's condition and it was making us uncomfortable.

There was something particularly strong and resolute in the boy's performance who emerged as the true hero of the play. All the punchlines were well-timed and they extracted the right reactions from the audience each time. The play was greatly appreciated and Abhay seemed relieved after it ended.

I couldn't resist myself from getting on the stage to tell the audience how unwell the boy was, and how well he had performed in his condition.

This play could not be called the best of its kind, but what we witnessed throughout was exceptional indeed. It reminded me of what Samuel Beckett had written, 'I Can't Go On, I'll Go On.'

The whole team got a standing ovation for their great improvisation skills and team spirit. Abhay was applauded for his determination and courage.

I quickly took the breathless boy to the specialist and got him nebulised.

He felt better and I took him back to the auditorium.

The 12-year-old, Abhay, was no longer an actor now. He pestered his parents to take him back to the hotel so that he could eat and sleep and be a child again.

Son

A bit too kind, a bit too calm
A world of cripples,
Devoid of it all,
Habits fair, ingrained since birth
Suddenly fade, into oblivion.

The MRI film was in front of me.

I could tell immediately, that the tumor had grown substantially but the knee still looked salvageable.

'Hmm, you have some kind of growth in your knee.'

'What does that mean?' Jasoda Devi asked with a grimace.

'Your knee is partly damaged.'

'What damage?'

'Didn't anyone tell you about the results of your MRI reports? Who did your MRI?' I asked.

'The doctor who did my MRI told me that it was a tumor. Is that so?'

She clasped her hands in dismay.

'Yes, it's a tumor, but nothing to really worry about. It's a treatable tumor,' I said reassuringly.

'No! Tumor is tumor! I know it!'

She suddenly began to cry, rendering her out of breath.

'Don't worry, it's not serious. It is not cancer, just a growth of some kind.'

I tried to make her understand.

'Believe me, I am like your son. I will not lie to you.'

She seemed more assured and relaxed, and stepped out of my cabin calmly agreeing to go ahead with the surgery.

Almost a week later, I operated on her. It was a difficult and lengthy operation as the tumor was very big and it had affected the main nerve too.

The next day, was one of the happiest days of Jasoda Devi's life as she was able to walk painlessly after a long time, albeit with support.

On the day of her discharge from the hospital I asked her 'So, aunty, you must be very happy to be finally going home!'

She remained silent.

'Aunty, are you fine?' I asked again.

She looked at me accusingly and said, 'What did you say to me on my first visit here? That you are like my son, right? Are you not?'

'Absolutely, I am just like your son,' I replied.

'You are not behaving like a son,' she said with dismay.

'The receptionist wants full payment from my son. He is an auto driver. While on his way here he got caught by the police and had to pay a fine of ₹500 rupees.'

'So you are upset with me?' I asked perplexed.

'Yes, why didn't you give me a discount?'

'I charged you the lowest amount possible which had already been discussed by us and you had agreed to pay it,' I said still confused.

'Then you shouldn't have said, that you're like my son,' she said, still angry.

I stood looking at her, speechless, until Ramesh, her son broke the silence, 'I apologise on behalf of my mother. Please check her dressings, Doctor. We are trying to manage our resources. Is it possible to pay the rest of the dues in installments when we come for the check-ups?' he asked pleadingly.

I opened the dressing, stitches looked neat and dry. Her wound was healing well.

Though I was satisfied with the outcome of my efforts yet my mind was in a turmoil.

'Be the kindhearted man you are. Can't you do it for charity? No, how can I… I have worked so hard… but it is for a worthy cause. Don't regret later! Do it! I battled with myself.

Sometimes it is difficult to distinguish between the virtues learnt in life that should be upheld and others that should be done away with.

While preparing the discharge papers I was smiling to myself and thinking that in the battle of the doctor versus the son, the son emerged victorious. Doesn't humanity always win?

A Blessing

Water the plant and take a glance
Or look away and miss the chance,
To watch it grow with flowers abloom
Or neglect and lead it to its doom.

'If you remove the wires, won't her bones get more weak?' Mr Hasan asked hesitantly.

'Her fracture has been corrected, don't worry. Just go and get it done,' I assured him.

He looked reluctant about the removal of the implant.

'Keep your hope alive. Without it, your heart will break, Mr Hasan.' I remarked gently.

When my assistant removed her wires, Umra reappeared, shrieking and chasing her father for a chocolate.

'I am grateful for all your help and we have been very fortunate to be treated by you.' Mr Hasan politely expressed his gratitude.

I nodded, but couldn't resist asking him, 'Is she the only

child you have? I have never seen anybody else from your family either, not even her mother.'

'Doctor, I actually have four children. One is married. The other is a spoiled brat, who doesn't listen to me. Honestly, it can't be helped anymore.'

'Umra is my third one. She was born following a complicated delivery by a local dai (midwife). Initially, she seemed to be in good shape but later, when she couldn't pass the key milestones like chewing solid foods and walking, we got worried. The specialist diagnosed her with cerebral palsy,' Mr Hasan sighed.

'She has always been very dear to my heart. Her vulnerability makes her even more lovable.

As a routine, she wakes up early in the morning, even before me, ready with her clothes and shoes. We go for a long walk. I have spent so many happy moments in my life with this girl, which cannot be described in mere words. There are not enough adjectives to describe the joy I feel when I'm with her.'

I felt a deep admiration for Mr Hasan for being such an affectionate father and raising a child with cerebral palsy. It's neither easy, nor common.

Every child is a blessing, the parents just have to accept and love their children, no matter how different they may be from others.

There for you

When you're sore and in pain
And your life seems to be in vain
I'll be there for you.
When you think you're a burden
And the shock comes so sudden
I will cry with you.
But when you think you're alone
And the cold chills you to the bone
I will be by your side
Till the end of time
With our hands intertwined
And our souls forever tied.

It was just another manic Monday and I had a hectic schedule. This has been going on for years and I can't imagine my life any other way.

While crossing the lobby, I noticed Ajay and Sujata's quiet presence.

They had returned after a long gap. Perhaps not a very prudent decision to discontinue the treatment for so long. Almost three months ago, Ajay had come to my clinic with a severely swollen wrist. He was also walking with the help of forearm crutches.

'Why do you use crutches?' I wanted to know.

An attack of polio at the age of four had left his lower right limb disabled. Suddenly, a loud voice caught my attention.

It was his wife.

'Can you see properly with your eyes?' I asked her.

'She went blind at the age of 19, sir', Ajay informed me.

I couldn't believe what I was hearing. My heart just melted.

How had they been managing their lives with so many limitations? I heard the story of their lives while going through Ajay's medical reports.

His mother had died three days after he was born and he had been brought up by his widowed aunt. At the age of four, Ajay experienced paralytic poliomyelitis. Not only did it immobilise him completely from the neck down, but it also attacked his lungs.

He was brought to Bareilly for his treatment.

'I still remember the face of that doctor, an absolute life saver'. he said.

'It was August, a popular month for polio and the wards were full of children. After a few weeks, both of my arms and my left leg recovered but my right leg did not. As soon as I was home from the hospital, I was sent off to the primary school, which I was utterly unprepared for, emotionally and physically. I had already missed the first six months of school, so I started off with a disadvantage.'

'Since then, the little complexities of life, would take over on many trivial occasions when I did not succeed at anything that I set out to do. My father was conspicuous by his absence and I can't tell you doctor, just how many difficulties I endured because of that. My Aunt took me to her maternal home, where I studied with my maternal cousins for company.'

I listened carefully.

'However, I had a special bond with Sujata, my cousin, since childhood. She cared for me and never mocked me for the way I walked, unlike others in the family. She was the eldest in the family and was more sensible and mature than the other children her age. We went to the same school and were in the same class. Those were the best days of my life. We were together most of the time and I learnt so many things from her. It is because of her tireless efforts that I'm standing in front of you today. Many times I was disheartened but she made me believe in myself. She was very determined and it was her courage and encouragement that gave me the strength to fight for myself.

'I remember when we were preparing for our high school board exams, she had difficulty studying during the night. Initially, I didn't realise the severity of the problem but when her eye sight didn't improve we went to Sitapur eye hospital for an eye check-up, where she was diagnosed with night blindness. Heavy supplements of Vitamin A also didn't help and retinitis pigmentosa set in later. Now, it was my turn to stand by her.'

With this sudden turn of events, I got even more engrossed in his story.

He went on, 'I wanted to marry her. Aunty was shocked when she first came to know about it. She was against the marriage. She tried to convince us otherwise by saying that Sujata was going to be permanently blind, without any chance of recovery.'

'Marriage between blood relatives is proscribed and seen as incest in Hindus,' said my Uncle. So we left my aunt's house and went back to live with my father who was old now and needed my help. I started working in a grocery shop. We got married, and tried to lead a happy life.'

'Almost a year ago, I noticed an unfamiliar pain in my wrist, a nasty twist. Is it because of my crutches?' Ajay asked more to himself than me.

'I have had many consultations since then. One of the doctors found a fault with my crutches, which I got corrected but it didn't help the pain at all. I consulted a few more doctors, but all in vain. It's been hurting immensely and gets worse in the middle of the night. I have heard a lot about you doctor, please treat me.' Ajay finally came to the point.

I remember, I had examined him thoroughly and finally advised an MRI.

'Would it cost too much?' his wife asked.

'No, I have already requested for a 50 per cent discount on your billing amount, so go and get it done.' I told them gently.

Looming granulomas studded his wrist in the MRI, directly indicating a tubercular wrist. The physician who was treating him earlier had rightly suspected tuberculosis and had given him anti-tubercular drugs, but the doses were inadequate. So I was dealing with a partially treated case with a secondary relapse.

Well, I had to advise the right line of treatment, regardless of their finances and I did. I told them that I would operate on him for free and they agreed to the surgery.

They never came back after that.

Three months later, I saw them sitting in the waiting lounge. I was eager to know why they had not come back for the surgery so I told my attendant to call them at the earliest.

They were a little hesitant to enter, looking crestfallen and silent in their misery. Something was amiss. I welcomed them with a smile, nevertheless.

I re-examined Ajay and I was dismayed by the condition of his wrist. It had become much worse.

'Why didn't you pay me a visit sooner? You are so irresponsible!' I had to vent my anger.

However, a part of me sympathised with them and I tried to calm myself down.

'Why didn't you come for the surgery, when I said I will do it for free?'

They looked at each other, and it was Ajay who finally spoke.

'During our first visit, Sujata was into eight months of her pregnancy. So, I had to postpone my surgery till she delivered. We had a beautiful baby boy and were so happy that I forgot all about myself. We named our baby Chirag, as his birth illuminated our lives. But God had other plans. A few days later, I noticed something amiss in his eyes and went to see a paediatric doctor and he told us that Chirag was congenitally blind.'

'We had to take him to AIIMS, Delhi. My son's surgery is scheduled for three months later so we decided to get my wrist operated on now.'

This is so unfair, I thought to myself. How can God be so heartless?

'What can I do for you?' I asked Ajay and Sujata.

'Just perform his surgery doctor, or whatever you think is right for him. I'll let you decide.' Sujata said.

'I'll do the best I can.'

As they left my office I couldn't help but admire their undaunting spirit and strength of character for facing up to everything that had befallen them. They not only met every challenge head-on but faced it with a smile. They were the true embodiment of hope and love. Love does conquer all.

Call my Name

If you feel alone,
Just call my name
I won't be there,
But I'll soothe your pain
I'll be your umbrella,
Whenever it rains
A mother just doesn't,
Leave her child in vain.

'A few months ago, you were worried sick about your son. Now you must be really happy. He's walking!' I said to Muneer's mother.

'Oh doctor, where else would I put my faith? I have nobody else in my life except him. His accident scared me out of my wits. You know, I lost his father in an accident too. Nobody knows what really happened, but when we found him, he was already dead and his body was lying in a hospital morgue,' she said. The atmosphere in the room suddenly became gloomy.

'I still have trouble coming to terms with it,' she continued. 'Muneer was born two months after his father's death. Who would know better than me the difficulties in raising a fatherless child in poverty? I didn't even have enough money to send him to school,' she said with tears in her eyes.

'Fortunately, he is very talented. At the tender age of ten, he started working in a tailoring shop; and at seventeen, he had mastered the art of dressmaking. He was soon employed by a big showroom where he would alter and sew clothes.' Muneer's mother looked at him adoringly.

'The accident threatened everything, his dreams, our lives; the future looked bleak.'

Muneer's mother broke down as she disclosed her life to me.

'But doctor, I was wrong. I was wrong to think like that. Because of you, he's walking again!' Her eyes began to glisten.

Sometimes as a doctor I carry the weight of expectations of my patients and their relatives on my shoulders, and it tends to drag me down but their faith in me and my belief in a higher power always helps me succeed.

It is only with the conviction of thoughts like these that I am able to make the gloom disappear.

A Second Chance

On that dreaded day,
The city echoed with screams.
With overflowing streams,
With broken dreams.
And even after so many tries,
Only a few were chosen
Amongst the cries.
A second chance at living,
in return for a thousand lives.

'I'm tired and in a foul mood because of these aches and pains doctor. Sometimes I feel it's my spine, or is it just my arthritis acting up?' Despite her problems, Mrs Gupta was smiling as usual.

'It's better to spend money, than to lose precious time. You can always get yourself examined, and see where the problem lies,' I said.

'Why should I waste money doctor? I believe you. You

are like God to me.'

'No no I'm far from God!' I replied. 'God doesn't need money but a doctor does.'

'Come on doctor, I paid eight thousand rupees in Kedarnath for the darshan.'

'Why?' I asked surprised.

'We were there in 2013, when because of the cloudburst, the entire area was submerged in water and the buildings got washed away causing numerous deaths and severe destruction.'

'Oh!'

'It has been half a decade since but for people like me, who witnessed the harrowing wrath of nature unfold, the tragedy remains a haunting memory.' Mrs Gupta continued.

'My relatives wondered if we were ever going to come back. It is true that the unparalleled scenes of death and destruction we witnessed have left us scarred forever. We came across a person who had lost 18 members of his family to the flood.'

'We went to the hallowed temple of our belief, but the calamity ruined the pilgrimage. I have seen the dark side of life but even in the darkest times, I have always believed, that the dark will give way to light. We were going to die, yet we got a second chance to live.

A few days later, it was another dawn. We reached our home and breathed a sigh of relief. We shed tears of joy on meeting our family members. All the pent up dread and fear dissipated on seeing them,' Mrs Gupta concluded.

I was surprised that Mrs Gupta, having survived such an ordeal, was so careless about her health.

'You're extremely lucky Mrs Gupta. People don't always get a second chance, but if you do, take advantage of it. It's better to spend money, than to lose time.' I was trying to make her understand.

How many of us appreciate the second chances that we get? I thought to myself.

'Please write a few medicines before I go,' she insisted, not paying heed to me.

'Of course I'll do that, but you know what William Osler said?'

'One of the first duties of the Physician is to educate the masses not to take medicine.'

After all prevention is better than cure.

Hope

Who's to say
I'm never gonna play?
If every dog has it's day
Then one may come
For the child of humans
Who lost his way.

'Will I ever stand straight on my feet; sometimes I wonder. You treated my fracture, even after the other doctors had given up on me,' said Jinshu, his gaze fixed on me with immense hope.

'"No point in treating him," Was what all the doctors said, until I met you. "He doesn't need any treatment for his fracture, he's crippled".'

The boy in front of me, just had one wish—to stand straight on his feet.

Jinshu knew it wasn't going to be easy. For as long as he could remember, he had never been able to walk. He was able to crawl on the floor somehow, but nothing more.

'My father took me to the district hospital, but they didn't give us any assurance or guidance.' He continued.

'My mother died three years ago. Since then, I am mostly alone. Sitting on a stone plinth, I watch school boys passing by during the day. A few of them have become my friends and we wave to each other every day. Of late, I have observed that my neck is getting stiff too and now I'm not able to watch the kites in the sky, not even if I tilt myself,' he said despondently.

'I need to talk to your father, and you need to go for an examination. Nothing is impossible, but it requires effort, a lot of hard work and money too,' I didn't want him to lose hope.

I told his father to consult my friend who is a rheumatologist.

'*Will I ever stand straight on my feet; sometimes I wonder,*' his words still haunt me.

I know that it is almost impossible for Jinshu to ever stand up straight again on his own, but I couldn't muster up the courage to tell him the truth.

I didn't have the heart to take away the only thing he had left: hope.

The Show Must Go On

All the chances I take
All the dreams I chase
I'm a believer.
All the words I recite
All the battles I fight
I'm a believer.
All the things I lose
All the things I gain
I'm a believer.
All the tears I shed
All the cheer I spread
I'm a believer.

With a heavy sigh, I was regretting my decision, when my theatre actor, who had performed for six consecutive days in the Ramleela, was admitted in hospital for hemorrhagic viral infection.

Why didn't I intervene on the first day itself? Why didn't

I suggest a replacement for him? Wasn't it totally inhuman to completely overlook a life, for the sake of our theatre? Why couldn't the show be cancelled, when a performing artist was bleeding before the show?

The organising committee, of which I was a member, couldn't imagine what it would be like to stage the show without Brijesh Tiwari.

We were obligated to hold shows for six consecutive days without interruption. Initially, he complained of nothing more than a high grade fever, he never once disclosed he was feeling unwell. His energy during the shows was surprisingly high.

Every evening, before the show, his fever would break and he would perform flawlessly. But every morning the fever would return.

His initial platelet counts were marginally low, so there was nothing serious to worry about.

A few hours before the last show, Brijesh had nasal bleeding, which deeply worried us all. However, not one to be easily disheartened, he performed his last show as Hanuman. There was a doctor behind the curtains, who was constantly keeping an eye on him.

The last show was as loudly applauded as the previous ones. During the final dinner, we were informed that his platelet count had gone down to alarmingly low levels and he had to be admitted to the intensive care unit.

'From the first day, I was down with high fever, but I knew I could do it. My love for acting has empowered me to live my character to the fullest. And all six days I was there, till the end.'

Brijesh smiled and said from his hospital bed.

Doctors are always taught to believe in science above all else, but I have noticed in my career, many times, that love and faith can work miracles, way beyond scientific reasoning. For Brijesh it was his love for theatre that carried him through. And here I can't help but think:

जा पर कृपा राम की होई ता पर कृपा करे सब कोई।
(Anyone who has been blessed by Lord Ram, is blessed by all.)

Road to Recovery

Deshpal was a 21-year-old boy from a poor family. He had come to me with an infected wrist and forearm. After looking at his reports, it became clear that what he had was a giant cell tumor, a kind that is locally malignant.

A local doctor in his district had tried to operate on it, but couldn't heal the wrist. As a result, his wrist had sinus discharge, which is when he came to me for treatment. I took on Deshpal as a challenge but later came to know of his weak financial background.

'It's my dominant hand doctor! I'm still young, and I need to work as I'm the eldest in my family. Moreover, I'm the only earning member. I have no father. I have to look after my family,' he said.

His words compelled me to think about it and I decided to give it a try. I assured him that I would save his wrist and forearm.

I started planning the surgery to be performed on Deshpal's wrist. During the process, I came to the realisation that the radial bone was directly touching the wrist. The infection ran deep and the joint had been completely destroyed.

I extracted the tumor but couldn't close the wound because of excessive bleeding. I filled it with pieces of gauze and put a bandage over it temporarily. I opened the dressing after 48 hours and cleaned it again. The process of opening and cleaning the dressing was repeated several times, resulting in a longer hospital stay.

I just couldn't understand how to heal his wrist. Finally, I decided to fix the upper bones with the bones of his hand. So, I fixed it and showed it to my plastic surgeon for further treatment. We applied vacuum suction to the wrist, following his advice, and then dressed the wound for a week.

After a week, when we opened the dressings again the condition was still not satisfactory so we closed it up again.. I had planned to insert a bone graft earlier but couldn't do that either because of the existing infection. After applying vacuum suction for the second time, I decided to discharge the patient.

Finally, Deshpal was discharged, but there was still a huge gap in his wrist bone. I thought I would fill it with a bone graft later. We decided that if everything turned out well in his follow up check- ups, we would fill the gap between the radius and his wrist.

I thoroughly explained to him and his family, the need and procedure of bone grafting.

'Everything seems to be fine for now, but we will do an MRI again. If, in the next few days, I find no reoccurrence of the tumor, I'll perform the bone grafting to stabilise your wrist. Minimising the possibility of the reoccurrence of the tumor is really important and so are the follow ups.'

After a few days, he came for a check-up but couldn't meet me. The junior doctor did his x-ray and sent him home. I didn't see him again.

Suddenly, after two years, Deshpal came to see me in my cabin. I greeted him heartily and asked about his wrist.

'I'm perfectly fine. I even ride a bicycle.' He said.

His hand movements were fairly good. I asked him to show me his old reports, but he had only come with an x-ray that I had not seen before. It had been taken a year ago, so I asked him to get another one done right away. I could then see the condition of his wrist, but he refused as he had no money. I told him that he could pay later, but he still refused to get it done.

'No I can't. There are people waiting for me outside who are giving me a ride back home.'

I urged him some more, trying to make him understand the importance of a follow up after recovery but he didn't listen and told me that he was even working now.

'How come you're riding now? You got the money for a bike?' I asked him.

'No, I'm not riding a bike. It's a bicycle.'

'Oh, that's fine.' I said.

He didn't have any reports with him and so I asked him to bring them along on his next visit.

'I need them not just for you but for my record as well.'

Deshpal said he would WhatsApp me the reports once he got home.

I needed to see the reports because I couldn't wrap my head around the fact that he had completely recovered without any further treatment or bone grafting.

Also, I couldn't help but wonder just how many patients in India do not go for follow-up care and recover on their own without proper treatment.

This is truly how incredible India is.

The Final Parting

Look o' look!
Your blood flows red
Burned with the lekythos
Your parting with the lack of those
Who sucked every ounce
Of you, and never renounced.
Look o' look!
You seem to be dead
Your pieces seep through
To the gargoyles you seemed to
admire, once you walked.
Scum clung to the mouth
Yet the bud still sprouts
In the darkest of places.
A swamp or a well
How beautiful and obnoxious
That life still dwells.
Does it make you wonder?

When the crows above screech
How Life is but a joke
And Death, but a shadow in the streets.

One

I will never forget 17 January 2014.

An early morning call woke me up and left me numb.

You were brought to the hospital. The Medical Officer on duty informed me.

'What did you say?' I asked twice, just to be sure.

'Yes sir,' the medical officer answered.

I rushed to the hospital with my heart pounding. I spotted you, my blue-eyed man, intubated and surrounded by monitors and doctors. They were trying their very best.

They had been willing your heart to beat, they had been willing your lungs to breathe.

Some were saying it was time.

I just couldn't give up. Not so soon.

Just a few more pumps.

Please God! Please breathe.

But you were getting weaker. Finally, I looked into your fading eyes and I wanted to cry.

I closed my eyes and took a deep breath.

I fell to my knees. Shaking uncontrollably.

My heart threatening to explode.

I sat on a bench outside, and saw your wife and mother praying silently with folded hands.

Your mother looked at me, with those eyes, your eyes. You have her eyes.

Those words. Those awful words. 'I'm so sorry.' I couldn't even say them.

'We did everything we could, but we could not save your son.'

Your mother fell to the floor and wrapped her frail arms around my legs. I nearly fell to the floor alongside her.

'Tell me it's not true, please tell me you're lying!' she screamed.

God! How I wish I was!

Every eye in the hospital was on us now.

To me, everything looked blurry as I sobbed uncontrollably. Your wife cried too.

She looked directly at me and said, 'Please bring him back, please bring my husband back!'

Everyone in the room was silent.

I brought them to where you lay.

Your mother held you in her arms, to her chest, near her heart, almost begging yours to beat.

'I'm so sorry', I cried with them. My heart bled with theirs.

Your mother looked at me with distant, empty eyes, your eyes. You had her eyes.

She whispered sadly, 'I just want him back, I want my son back.'

Time stood still.

God, how I wish I could bring you back. How I wish I could undo everything, give her back her blue-eyed son.

Instead, I give you me.

You lived with our family for 20 years, my best friend, my partner in crime, my confidante. Your children will have me, as a second father. Your mother will have me, as a second son.

Forever

Always.

Two

One day, in your 86th year, you slipped and fell.

You fractured your hip. Your family was told that surgery would be good for you.

But it was not.

You bravely withstood the procedure, but the after effects took their toll on your frail body and emotions.

Recuperation was a struggle for you. Your spirit also aged. You found it very difficult to even cough. You became weaker and weaker.

We rushed you back to the Surgical- Intensive-Care. Your blood pressure fell drastically.

Your kidneys had given up. Your liver was affected. Your skin had turned a jaundiced yellow.

They got in touch with your darling son.

The doctors informed him that your body was septic and you were fading away from life.

In your critical hours, you would mumble incoherently and, the next moment, speak with vivid clarity.

It was as if you were playing hide-and-seek with life and death.

You believed your loved ones would stay and help you survive. After all, your son and daughter-in-law were both doctors.

One could hear you mumble. It seemed as if you were prepared for death. After all, you were 86.

You led a wonderful life. You had 60 wonderful years of marriage.

As a doctor, I had to inform your family that your organs were failing. The lungs, the kidneys and the liver were giving up.

That night, you wanted your family to stay with you. Perhaps, you wanted to hear their voices or perhaps you wanted them to hear yours.

Perhaps, you wanted to remember all the meaningful moments in your life your marriage, the birth of your children, and the birth of your—grand children. Perhaps, for the last time, you wanted to talk about your two favorite movies, 'Anand' and 'Abhimaan'.

Perhaps, you wanted to meet the youngest doctor in your family, your grand-daughter, and cradle her in your arms, just like you cradled her as a child.

You waited for your family before the comforting arms of death embraced you. But they didn't come.

They left, promising to be back in the morning.

You were left with a tube in your lungs and a machine to breathe for you. You were injected with many drugs just to keep you alive. Your life was our prized possession and we did our best to save it.

But then, you slipped into a coma that night. Some hours before that, you were talking to us. If your family had been there, they could have joined in the conversation. Perhaps you could have shared a little laugh, held each others' hands in a union, celebrating life.

But they were not there.

They came the next day. By then you were gone.

If only you could have held hands with your loved ones, one last time, just before the last breath left your body.

If only…

Three

It was one of the more hectic operating nights.

When I got a little respite, I excitedly said to my night anesthetic Dr Sandeep, 'Hey Sandeep, I am so excited about Dr Paul Kalanithi's new book. His posthumous memoir, 'When Breath Becomes Air.'

I had been an ardent fan and follower of Dr Kalanithi's writings, essays and reflections.

What was most pertinent and motivational about this exceptional doctor's short- lived life, was his own tryst with cancer.

He was diagnosed with stage IV lung cancer in 2013, though he never smoked. As a doctor, he understood the disease and described it in terms of clinical philosophy. His essays for *The New York Times* and *Stanford Medicine* were reflections of a physician and also that of a patient's. He wrote on the human experience of facing death and the joy he found despite his terminal illness.

He wrote most eloquently and movingly about facing his own mortality.

I would read his notes, his writings, during the breaks I would get in course of my own hectic practice. Through his writings, I saw him as a person who lived with great dignity both as a doctor and as a cancer patient. For me he was the hero of all heroes. He taught me that respectful communication is the bedrock of all medicine.

Dr Sandeep and I would often share notes from Dr Kalanithi's writings.

One day, Dr Sandeep came out with his own story. I was awestruck by the narrative.

It was around 2001 when Dr Sandeep was working with Gangaram Hospital in New Delhi.

His mother had a recurrence of her nasopharyngeal carcinoma. The scenario was very dismal. They had met with several oncologists and most were wary of recommending the second line of drugs because of their toxicity.

Dr Sandeep was disheartened. His Head of Department (HoD) could sense his dismay, and so he advised him to meet Dr D.C. Doval of Rajiv Gandhi Cancer Institute (RGCI) with the reference of Dr Raman Chaddha who was the HoD of anaesthesia at RGCI.

'I gathered my strength and visited RGCI. It came as no surprise that the hospital was crowded with patients and the doctors were very busy. In the corridor outside the operation theatre, I located Dr Raman Chaddha who looked so jovial and exuberant, even amidst his hectic schedule.' Dr Sandeep recalled.

'I forwarded Dr Kumar's reference letter, it explained the purpose of my visit. Dr Chaddha welcomed me and asked me to sit as he glanced through the letter.

'"No problem! We will go over to Dr Doval's office," Dr Chaddha amiably, reassured me.'

Dr Doval turned out to be as friendly and obliging as Dr Chaddha. He explained to Dr Sandeep, the pros and cons of a second line of chemotherapy.

Dr Sandeep vividly remembered that meeting of 2001, that marked a turning point in his mother's cancer treatment. That meeting cleared his doubts and confusions. He now set out to plan her treatment. The chemotherapy treatment was on course.

Thereafter, he did not meet Dr Doval at RGCI and returned to his work at Gangaram Hospital.

A few months later, one evening, Dr Sandeep got a call at home from Dr Kumra, 'Please do not forget to do a PAC (pre-anesthetic check-up) of Dr Raman Chaddha. He got late for his admission and is scheduled for surgery early morning tomorrow.'

Dr Sandeep wondered whether he was the same doctor whom he had met at RGCI.

'I drove straight to Gangaram Hospital. In front of me, was the same welcoming smile of Dr Chaddha who was now covered with tubes.'

'How is your mother doing?' The doctor asked from his bed.

'Do you still remember sir?' Dr Sandeep was surprised.

'Yes, I do.'

'What happened sir? What surgery are you scheduled for tomorrow?'

Dr Sandeep had not had the time to check the case-sheet. His curiosity prompted him to ask many questions.

'It's nothing serious,' Dr Chaddha said, casually trying to brush away Dr Sandeep's anxiety.

The latter then looked at the reports and his heart sank. It was cancer.

Dr Chaddha's experienced eyes read Dr Sandeep's perplexity and quipped, 'Do you know that by dying young, a person always stays young in people's memories. So I may die, but I'll never get old. Isn't it?'

Words failed Dr Sandeep.

'I just about managed to say, "What are you saying sir?"'

But Dr Chaddha changed the topic instead.

'You tell me your future plans. Which city do you want to settle down in?'

Dr Sandeep continued with his concern. 'Sir, are you not worried about the surgery?'

'None of us are exempt from going under the surgical knife at some stage in our lives. It is my turn now. What is wrong with being a patient and undergoing a surgery? Moreover, I have the comfort of all of you being around to support me and cheer me up,' he replied.

Dr Sandeep barely manage to mumble, 'True sir, there's nothing wrong about being a patient. It can happen to anyone.'

Later while recalling the story, Dr Sandeep reflected, 'Being a doctor is all about having control and yet wielding power. Being a patient, and that too of cancer, is all about losing control and feeling utterly vulnerable. Who knows that better than me?'

Dr Chaddha then went on to explain his symptoms.

'Over the last few months, I noticed a drastic weight loss. I also developed night sweats and an unbearable back pain. I thought it was a result of working continuously. Moreover, I was not a smoker so I did not correlate the symptoms to cancer.'

Upon examination, it was revealed that one of the lungs was infiltrated, even though not impaired. A lobectomy (excision of an organ or gland) was planned. The operating team hoped that metastasis (the transference of disease-producing organisms from one part of the body to another) would not have set in yet. His spine looked normal even though he had severe back pain.

Before taking his leave, Dr Sandeep ascertained that Dr Chaddha's PAC was near normal. He encouragingly remarked, 'Please do not worry sir. Your surgery will be a great success. Have a good sleep and do take your tranquiliser.' Dr Sandeep then bid adieu.

The next morning, when Dr Sandeep joined the team, Dr Raman Chaddha had already been brought into the OT and tranquilised.

He recalled, 'The surgery was a difficult one and took a long time. Upon its completion, I moved on to other work and lost track of the case as I was not supposed to visit him clinically.'

One hot afternoon in May 2001, he was informed of Dr Chadda's death by a colleague.

'I spent the whole day reflecting upon the unfairness of death, to take a life so young.

Both Dr Sandeep and I often reflect upon the philosophy of life and death. Many die young yet continue to live vividly in the memories of those they leave behind. Their loved ones continue to draw strength from the immortal spirit. They continue to inspire the living.

Dr Chaddha's reflections and attitude towards cancer and death added to the nobility of his character and his profession. In my profession, I have also had the privilege to meet may people whose attitude toward life continues to inspire me even after their death.

Nothing Can Stop You Now

Blue is for sky
The horse is so high

Red is for apple
My seat's on the saddle

Green is for tree
I carry on my spree

Purple is for flowers
I watch them for hours

Yellow is for sun
It makes my eyes burn

Orange is for orange
This can never get boring

Priyansh appeared less shy today, with his folder of drawings beside his prescription.

I recalled the last time that he visited, I had enquired of his schedule and wanted to know if he was keeping himself constructively occupied during his vacations.

'He keeps busy with his drawings, besides plotting mischief. He always gets into altercations with his sister,' his mother complained, albeit indulgently.

As I turned my head to look at him, I realised that he always had an irrepressible, mischievous smile etched on his face.

'Whenever he sees a white piece of paper, he gets tempted to draw on it. He's a great storyteller. It is through his many drawings that we discover what he really wants to say,' his father said enthusiastically.

'Would you like to see my drawings?' Priyansh mumbled, holding up his injured hand, which had started to heal.

'Yes, of course!' I replied.

I was astonished by the amount of raw talent the boy had at such a young age.

'Sensational! Are these sketches really made by you?' I asked in awe.

'Yes,' the boy replied with a beaming smile.

'Believe me, these are so captivating, drawn as realistically as possible from his viewpoint and perspective. His skills are beyond his age,' I praised him to his parents.

Today we have a lot of new, computerised technologies available for drawing. However, drawing made with pencil on paper remains the most beautiful form of art for me, by far.

'Do you know what else you need now?' Priyansh listened to me attentively, as I remarked, 'Easels, palettes, canvasses, oil pastels, water colours, sketch pads, pencil sets, brushes—virtually anything an artist would need. You should have them all.' I suggested to his father.

'Let him spread the wings of his imagination and paint the canvas of his own sky with the brightest of colours,' I said to his proud parents.

'Nothing can stop him now! Nothing should stop him now!'

Ma

Ma, I know you're scared, and so am I
But don't leave just yet
Without you, who am I?
As you turned grey,
And your voice started to fail
I sat in front of God
To whom, you always prayed
For my health and success
And all the world's happiness, nothing less!
If only you had asked,
A little bit for yourself
Then maybe you wouldn't have to go
Much sooner than myself.

Let me hold onto you just a bit longer
Let me carve into my memory
The way your hands feel
Against my temple and my cheeks
And reminisce the same

In the cold, when I shudder.
And when you're no longer here
But just your lingering scent in the air
Cocooning me gently,
I'll be reminded of your hair
cascading over my head, forming a lair
Lulling me to sleep
To have your sweet dreams.

I find you everywhere
You're a part of my being
And it's so unfair
That while I walk the earth
And carry you forever in my heart
You won't be by my side
Like you've never even been.
I swear to God, that if I could,
I'd bargain everything precious
To make you stay with me
And if your God says otherwise,
I'd call the Devil to seal the deal.

So please, won't you just stay with me?
Your son's a sorry excuse
For all you've ever been.
I will listen to everything you say
And I promise to follow your way
I'll sleep on time, I'll eat on time
And I'll complete my chores everyday.
But for the sake of me and a simple prayer

For as long as I'm there,
Ma, won't you just stay?

My friend had been crying in grief. My friend is affectionately called 'S' by everyone.

S has helped save many lives inside the operation theatre and also accomplished many successful surgeries. Ours is not only a professional relationship but a personal one as well.

He is my childhood friend but we are more like brothers. Seeing him cry, I was overcome with grief.

A doctor, who helped save the lives of hundreds of patients, had his own mother breathe her last in his lap. His mother had been sick for a long time but was recovering slowly.

On a Sunday morning, she ended up with a morsel of food, stuck in her throat.

He tried everything he could to extract it from her throat at home and even rushed her to the hospital.

'It was hard to see her turning blue and slip away in my arms and I just looked on helplessly, unable to do anything.' S told me sadly.

Ever since he was a child his mother had been sick quite frequently. She had asthma and was allergic to a lot of things. She was especially allergic and sensitive to strong smells of incense and perfumes. Cold water did not agree with her. Even in the hot summer months she would bathe with lukewarm water.

After completing his MD, S had joined one of the most reputed hospitals in Delhi.

S told me, 'It was around that time, that Ma got diagnosed with nasopharyngeal cancer. After a lot of chemo and radio therapies, she was almost cured. The whole family was overjoyed. But soon, Ma's sense of taste and hearing started to falter.'

S's parents had been living together happily for years, until his mother got bedridden.

His father devoted the rest of his life to looking after his wife. He would not leave the house for anything, not even to pray at the nearest temple.

Ma was very fond of S, he would spend several hours with her every day after he returned from the hospital. He avoided using perfume or deodorant so as not to aggravate his mother's allergy. They both shared a special bond.

S had almost stopped going out socially, though he would meet me twice a week. We would always speak of his mother and I would often wonder at his devotion and love for her. My respect for him reached new heights.

I had last met S's mother a month ago. I had bought a new car and driven to his house. Aunty gave me her love and blessings.

Suddenly, when the news of her death reached me, my first thought was of S.

He was always thinking about her when she was alive and now that she was no more, how would he react to her passing?

It is so surreal and emotionally challenging to hand over one of your own to the funeral-pyre, to cremate your own. I usually avoid going to the crematorium, but this time around I had to go.

Aunty had been very dear to me since childhood. She was as beautiful inside as she was on the outside. Now seeing her dead body, I was overcome with emotion and tears. I noticed S constantly wiping his eyes with his handkerchief throughout the day while he sat by his mother's body, holding her lifeless hand.

The next day, when I called him, he couldn't hold back his tears and cried profusely.

'You see S, death does not always comply with our wishes or plans. You will overcome this but it will take time.' I tried to console him.

'No Vijji, time does not heal all wounds. I don't think the pain ever really goes away,' he said.

I agreed with him and told S how the pain of my father's death had never left me.

As he started to dwell on his late mother again, his voice cracked. He recalled how he used to hold his mother's hand for hours. He also recalled how she would always tell his wife, 'Beta, when I die, do not bathe me with cold water and do not keep any incense-sticks near my pyre.'

S told me that Aunty was fed up with her bedridden life but she lived only for him.

Hey S,

The pain of loss is a reflection of our love. Love never dies, love transcends all. In fact, you may find that you love her more than you ever did before. She will always be with you in your heart.

We are the ones who have perpetuated the belief that we are superhuman, infallible to illnesses that plague others.

However, as doctors, we are allowed to be physically or mentally ill. We are allowed to grieve. How will we ever heal others if we don't allow ourselves to heal? We are, after all, human beings first.

Guilty

Guilty or not
It's for the world to judge
Innocent may you be
Guilty for some
This world never sees
The suffering and darkness
Some have to face
In the name of justice

It had taken me more than a year to get Sartaz back on his feet, walking without support.

I remember his first visit, limping slightly and smiling as he walked into my chamber. He must have been 40, though he looked older than his years.

After looking at the X-rays and the condition of his limb, I asked him,

'Why haven't you been to a good orthopedic doctor till now? It's been 12 years and your fracture hasn't healed, it is infected too, and may get even worse.' His family looked at me with expressions of sorrow and hope on their faces.

'That is the reason I have come to you sir,' he said resolutely.

The court has granted me special permission to get my leg treated and they will verify the same. I have already informed them about you. I have been in custodial remand for the last 28 months. One of the judges recognised my worsening condition and permitted me to get myself cured.'

'Why did you go to Tihar?' I asked.

'I have been accused of drug trafficking, but haven't been convicted.'

'Are you guilty?' I asked with a frown.

He looked down and his eyes grew misty.

'I fell into a trap. That was my fault.'

How many like him are trapped? I thought to myself but I had no time to reflect on it as there was a large number of patients waiting to be seen by me.

'See Sartaz, I shall do whatever needs to be done to save your limb but do not neglect it any further. Another important thing you must note is that it might take a long hospitalisation and it may cost you a fortune. It depends on the number of surgeries required, which can only be ascertained once your first surgery has been performed. Nonetheless, your condition will definitely get better,' I said.

Sartaz and his wife readily agreed to everything I said. It was a surprise to me, as patients and their relatives usually bargain over the cost involved in the treatments.

Sartaz got admitted on the scheduled date. The same

night, he was taken for his first surgery. I had to remove his infected implant and clean the bone as much as possible. He had multiple discharging sinuses.

'Where did you get this surgery done?' I asked.

He didn't answer.

'Do you drink alcohol?' the anaesthetist asked.

'Sir, it's *haram* (prohibited) in Islam,' he replied confidently.

'Then any kind of drugs? You were caught for drug trafficking after all,' I asked him.

'No sir, not at all.' He replied with a trace of irritation in his voice.

'I had gone to Safdarjung Hospital for three surgeries. It was in 2007, twelve years ago.'

'Do you work in Delhi?' I asked.

He didn't answer straight away but then slowly began to narrate his ordeal.

*

'I was driving a truck in Gurugram, when I met with a near-fatal accident. I suffered a severe head injury and my limbs were fractured. I remained unconscious for more than two months. Later, I underwent several limb surgeries. The surgeries caused a shortening of my limb. Another surgery was performed to get the limb lengthened but it got infected. Since then, the infection has never healed.

Despite that, I started driving my truck again. I did not have the money or the luxury of not working, I have a family to feed. I was able to walk, so I decided to delay any further surgeries which I might have required.

Until I was ten years old, my family had lived in a city but we moved back to the village after my father's sudden demise. During that time, I learned how to cut, bend and solder wire to make silver jewellery. I was also working in a garment shop in the city, commuting from my home to work and vice-versa every day. It was down to me to look after the family with an invalid mother and an unmarried sister.

My struggle lasted for years, till I started driving a truck. My wife and sister also started working in a garment company. We worked very hard to make ends meet. Life was always a challenge and the birth of my third daughter made it more difficult. We wanted a boy who would support us in our old age.

In Shahjahanpur, our hometown, many people are involved in the heroin business and they make a lot of money. The potential heroin yield from our districts is estimated to be in billions. Until I went to jail, I had an unblemished reputation. I always kept myself away from drugs.

Then one day, when I was sitting in an over-crowded train, all of a sudden, my arms were seized and locked into iron cuffs by the Delhi Police. My voice trembled and tears ran down my face as I pleaded to be released. I was arrested and taken to Delhi. I was charged for being involved in delivering morphine to different destinations.

The next day was a holiday and I was made to appear in a judge's house and then, was taken on remand from there. I was not sure of the duration of my remand but I was sure that I was going to spend my nights behind bars.

Why was I kept on remand? That was the question.

Since I was in jail for a long time, my infection got aggravated, so, I requested the jail authorities to arrange for my treatment. My cellmate was a doctor who convinced the jail authorities that I needed urgent treatment and thus I was given medical leave after 28 months in jail.

❦

After several interventions, including prolonged hospitalisation, surgeries, and continual care from our team of specialists, Sartaz started improving.

Despite the fear of going back to prison, he always had a cheerful disposition. He never complained or troubled any staff member. During the period of Sartaz's treatment and hospitalisation, I constantly received queries regarding his progress from the police.

I never thought of him as a criminal, but only as a fellow human being in need of my help.

One busy afternoon, a person from the Delhi Police Special Cell, Narcotic Drugs and Psychotropic Substances (NDPS) came to see me. He said,' Sir, we have been receiving a lot of letters about Sartaz so I decided to talk to you personally regarding his actual condition.' Did you allow him to ride a bike?' He asked.

'No, he's advised to just walk that too with support only.' I replied.

'What do you think doctor? How much time until he is completely healed? You won't allow him to go before that, will you?'

'Three months.' I answered. 'After that, he has to face

imprisonment, right? I feel bad for all those innocent people who are in jail, just like Sartaz.'

'We can't imprison anybody on suspicion alone doctor. Sartaz is playing innocent in front of you. We have enough proof that he is a drug trafficker,' he said.

I wasn't ready to believe it though.

'As an investigating officer, I know it's your duty to say that.'

'You know nothing sir. 69 kg of high-grade opium, worth crores in the international market was recovered from his truck. Sartaz was among four accused of being part of an inter-state drug traffickers cartel. In this regard, a case has been registered at PS Special Cell, Delhi. They used to transport illegal drugs from Nagaland and other North-Eastern States to Punjab via UP, Delhi and NCR. They had been under our surveillance for six months before we arrested them. That's how they were caught in Nand Nagri, Delhi, around 7.00 p.m., they were caught exchanging the contraband', he concluded.

I always take people on face value and everyone seems kind and innocent. Once you start learning more about the world, you realise people can be very selfish and mean. They are often worse than you can ever imagine.

After the police officer was gone, I was not so sure of Sartaz's innocence anymore.

On the next follow-up, Sartaz's X-ray showed that his injury was healing well.

'Good for you! It's a great achievement.' I congratulated Sartaz.

'Those 28 months in jail felt like 28 years, but these

14 months just flew by. In a way, I'm happy. I shall now concentrate on getting bail and proving my innocence in a court of law,' he said.

Everyone in my cabin was silent.

'It's time to say goodbye sir I'm very grateful for all the time and care you have given me. Time to get back to life.'

Sartaz took his x-ray and went out to face whatever life had in store for him.

As he was leaving, my cabin was plunged into darkness by a sudden power outage, perhaps heralding what lay ahead for him.

Prelude

My love, do you see?
Without you, life is a misery.
You did, but my love shall never die
Move on, I will
Unto you, I can never lie.
That while you're gone
With the world's rules, I shall comply
Though the hearts are dead, yours and mine
In a galaxy far, my dear, they'll again unify.

'How long will it take, doctor? It's already been three months!' Sachin looked at his limb with dismay. 'I have two children to look after. Though my mother helps me out, she has not been keeping well these days,' he said with concern in his voice.

'Why does your mother help you? 'I asked.

'Don't you remember my accident, sir?' he said

'Oh, sorry… I do remember.' I said.

'My shop has been closed for the past three months. Tell me, how do I cope under such difficult circumstances and the challenges that lie ahead?'

I turned on the overhead light and examined his X-rays and injuries again, calming him down.

'As I passed my high school exam, I started earning because I had responsibilities.'

'If you want to earn more, learn more,' my father always said, so I joined computer classes. I was young and naïve and fell in love with my computer teacher, Nalini. It was love at first sight.

Initially she thought I was just infatuated by her but she soon realised that I truly loved her. A deep mutual respect and understanding developed between us. We decided to get married.

She was a Sikh girl and I belonged to a conservative Hindu family. She changed herself completely. She quit wearing jeans, looking even more beautiful in saris and a bindi, as per the wishes of my family. We got married and settled down.

She started visiting temples and I accompanied her to gurudwaras. I came to like the Nagarkeertans l attended. We were living in the most peaceful area of our city, which had a famous temple. Every evening the entire colony reverberated with the sounds of dhopa temple bells and this was our time to visit and participate in the aarti.

One evening while lighting diyas, I heard the most horrifying shrieks of my life. As I turned towards the source of the sound I shuddered in fright. My wife's clothes were on fire, she was screaming, and running out of the house towards the temple. I ran after her to stop her. I caught up with her and made her lie down on the temple floor. The chanting inside the temple stopped and we were surrounded by a crowd of people.

For a while she was kept in the nearby hospital. Doctors informed us that she had 50 per cent burns and recommended plastic surgery. Even after three days of intensive care, she was not out of the woods.

This was an emotional injury as well; we were suffering as a family. There was nothing any one of us could do but to endure the pain. I knew I could not let the circumstances defeat me. I had courage to fight for my love till the last breath.

We shifted her to a better nursing home, but it was way beyond our means. The financial burden was increasing and family and friends had also stopped helping. So, I had to shift her treatment to Bijnor, as suggested by some of our relatives. This turned out to be a cheaper and more effective option. We started commuting in an ambulance to Bijnor daily.

One morning, I woke up in a hospital bed bound in bandages and plasters. I remembered nothing of how I got there or what had happened to me.

'Where is my family, my wife?'

'She is also injured', my brother told me. 'Your van met with an accident.' But I couldn't react and fell unconscious again for a long time

My eyes opened in the crematorium. My wife had been killed during the accident, she never made it alive to the hospital.

I was on a stretcher, reflecting on how you saved my limbs

and my life doctor, but I feel disabled. I couldn't help her in her last moments, I couldn't be of any comfort to her.

No one can imagine the gut-wrenching, heart-breaking turmoil and confusion which I have been living with in these past days in my hospital bed. 'I can barely remember a time I did not want her, did not need her, did not adore her.'

'Now everything has changed,' Sachin cried in frustration.

'Yes, it gets complicated sometimes,' I barely managed to whisper after listening to his ordeal.

'I have no idea where to go or what to do from here.

I feel like I have plunged into a wide open abyss with nowhere to escape.'

'Sometimes when you lose your way, you find yourself. They say that when life closes one door it opens many others and it is up to us make the most of it.'

'Yes doctor, I have come to the point in my life from where I have to start all over again. I have to live for my children, our children. I have to find Nalini in my daughter's smile, I have to look for her in my son's courage. I have to keep her memory alive for all of us.

'Yes, absolutely!'

The soul is healed by being with children, Fyodor Dostoevsky had rightly said. I smiled and called for my next patient.

Gunjan

'Gunjan' (गुंजन) is the sound emanating from a beehive, the sound of bees humming. It carries its own promise of sweetness and a sting.

A doctor's life also carries the same, the sweetness and sting of experiences he or she lives individually and with all the patients in his or her life. The echo, the resonance of medical cases and experiences continue to reside in your memory and heart.

One day, on a hot summer afternoon, I walked into my hospital's OPD chamber. For me it is not out of the ordinary to find a very long line of patients waiting for me. By the time I attend to them and call it a day, it is well past evening. Like most doctors I have met a sea of people, as it were. Patients come, get treated and leave. Although some patients remain in our memories forever. This is the story of Gunjan, one such patient.

One day, a beautiful young girl of around twenty walked into my chamber. She was suffering from an acute pain in the hip. She was accompanied by her mother, a very talkative woman, and her brother, who was equally effervescent. Gunjan's brother informed me that they had consulted many doctors before me, but to no avail. Someone had given them my reference. He also showed me a long list of medical diagnoses, and prescriptions from a number of doctors. This itself revealed to me that Gunjan had already undergone a lot of treatment.

I examined Gunjan and told them to get an MRI. The MRI report informed me that she had a reduced blood flow in both her hip bones. Gunjan had developed AVN (Avascular Necrosis of hip). It is a very painful condition. It usually gets diagnosed late by clinicians as the patients themselves cannot comprehend the severity of the pain or the need for immediacy of it being attended to. In Gunjan's case, there had been a delay in getting proper treatment. Gunjan and her family had neglected the initial pain in her hips. Consultations with local doctors and neurologists could not address the issue. The passage of time had also resulted in making the condition more severe. In such cases a total hip replacement is the way forward.

'She is too young doctor, and not even married,' said the mother. The mother and brother were more preoccupied with Gunjan's marital prospects rather than her physical well-being. As a doctor, I have experienced that people in rural India still shy away from getting a hip-replacement surgery done. They are either not mentally prepared for it, or, cannot afford a lifestyle change that such a surgery entails. Post a hip-replacement surgery, sitting and squatting on the floor is difficult and the rural domestic lifestyle often makes this equally difficult.

Seeing their adverse reaction to the hip-replacement surgery, I suggested another medical intervention called the core-decompression-surgery which is performed with a small incision. The attempt is to save the hips, but generally the procedure has a low success rate. I suggested a few other treatment options but, considering they were all surgeries, none appealed to them.

I tried to reason with and counsel Gunjan. 'Look if you are experiencing hip issues, no matter what your age, be open to the idea of a replacement or to the other hip- saving procedures. 'If something goes wrong in your life, it is best to acknowledge it quickly and find a solution.' I even told them to consult other doctors if they had any doubts about my suggested treatment advice.

After consulting a few more doctors the family came back to me. However, they were still reluctant to let Gunjan undergo a hip-replacement surgery. Marriage proposals were coming in plenty and her physical problem was to be kept a secret from the society. Getting her married was more important than undertaking a crucial surgery. The mother and brother loved Gunjan, but the limitation of their clinical knowledge made them very ignorant. They had been told repeatedly that medicines or rest would not solve the problem. They finally opted for Gunjan to undergo the core-decompression-surgery, the small incision surgery that I had suggested as an alternative to hip-replacement, even though I had warned them that the results were not very promising. The surgery was done. They were informed that, post surgery, a three-month bed rest was mandatory for Gunjan and she was to not let her legs bear any weight at all.

The biggest challenge was that Gunjan and her family were reluctant to abide by the post-operative care, which is imperative for recovery. Post-operative dos and don'ts were not adhered to. My advice, even warnings, went unheeded. At the hospital we gave her the best medical-care and physiotherapy. She started walking easily. There was also some relief from the pain. Then suddenly, she stopped coming for therapy and disappeared altogether.

Some months passed and then one day, just as she had disappeared, Gunjan reappeared at my clinic. This time she was on a wheelchair accompanied by her family. She was in severe pain. I learnt that soon after she had discontinued her physiotherapy with us she had got back to doing all the strenuous household chores, despite our advice. The toilet in her house was the Indian, squatting one. Besides, she would also squat and wash utensils, sweep and mop the house. As a result her hip had collapsed. The x-ray was not favourable. I was furious.

Medicines were not going to be of any help now. There was no other way to treat Gunjan but with a hip replacement. I suggested that she and her family go to Delhi and consult a good joint-replacement surgeon. They were reluctant. I tried to impress upon them that her quality of life depended on further treatment, otherwise she would be on a wheelchair for the rest of her life. I continued with my persistent advice, 'Look, this is not an old person who is afflicted, but a young one who has an active life ahead. The need for hip replacements is growing every year. What's even more surprising is that the average age for the surgery is changing as well. Even people in their twenties are getting the surgery nowadays. Many young and active people run the risk of hip arthritis following an AVN hip.' I tried to convince them. However, against my best advice they continued to treat it with medicines and refused surgery.

After a few months, Gunjan reappeared in my clinic again, along with her mother and brother. She looked beautiful and wore the look of someone who had married recently. I smiled and remarked 'I'm surprised to see you here. Did you get married?'

Gunjan was beaming. She said 'Yes. I am happy. My family is very nice.'

She had been married for a month. I asked her if she had told her husband and in-laws about the problem in her hip.

Gunjan said,' No, I am not going to tell them, doctor. I'm doing all the household chores with help from a maid. However, there are some issues. I can walk, but can't keep up with my husband who walks very briskly. I can stay up for a party till late in the night but can't dance with my husband although he loves dancing. My husband enjoys biking too, but I can't join him. My father-in-law wants me to do yoga with him, but I have been successful in avoiding it till now.'

'So you are managing it this way, by pretending that there isn't a problem. The bigger question is, for how long?' I asked her.

Gunjan replied: 'Yes doctor,' and hesitated before

confessing, 'The most critical thing is that I can't open my thighs wide. It really hurts.'

I understood what Gunjan, a married woman wanted to communicate, but could not discuss openly. She pleaded, 'I just want this to be corrected, doctor. My husband insists that I consult an orthopaedic doctor, who happens to be his friend, but I am trying to avoid it since I don't want him to know about my preexisting condition. My marriage is now under threat. How do I tell him the truth?'

This was my advice to her: 'Lies and secrets are like non-healing wounds. They only leave behind pain and mistrust. There comes a point in every person's life when they need medical or surgical intervention or a device, whether it's glasses, contacts, joint replacement or a pacemaker. The prosthetic generation is all around us. So don't worry. Motivate yourself to tell him the truth. You can hide your physical shortcomings from the world, but not from a conjugal partner. You can camouflage facial or body defects with make-up, cover-up the scars, but not such a disability. We reveal ourselves more by what we try to hide.'

I don't know if I had convinced her to tell her husband the truth.

To convince her for surgery itself had been a challenge. Precious time had been wasted. She had managed six years of active life, before getting married. But now she was at a point in life that asked for a very challenging choice to be made. It was morally, ethically and conjugally imperative that she gather the courage to tell her husband the truth. This was my advice. This newly married girl was carrying a secret, which was weighing heavily on her marital life.

Almost six weeks later, one evening when I was in Davos for a conference, I got to know that Gunjan and her husband had met with an accident. It had left her husband with a cracked rib and a shattered pelvis. Gunjan had escaped with just a few scratches. Her husband had to undergo a surgery to repair his pelvis but that could leave him at high risk of an AVN hip, which could only be prevented by a hip replacement surgery.

Now Gunjan became both hopeful and confident at the same time. She was convinced that her husband would forgive her for hiding the truth from him all along, since he himself was going through the same thing. She was confident that together they would overcome all their problems. She never contacted me after that and I don't know if she ever told her husband the truth. And if she did, did he understand and forgive her?

Treating a patient like Gunjan is a lesson in a larger context too. It makes you aware of your deeply-rooted social-cultural-gender biases that especially challenge Indian women and their place in marriage or society. Wounds that go beyond the physical need to be acknowledged. Men need to address this adverse social conditioning. Men need to empathise and be more supportive of their wives and daughters. They need to be the change.

The Survivor's Lament

October 2017

Shikhar, a young entrepreneur from an elite background, was brought to us in a serious condition. He was completely unconscious, with a broken jaw and shattered limbs, following a road accident a day before Diwali. It was around 1 a.m., if I recall correctly. He was severely injured and was bleeding profusely, which made his condition near fatal. His air passages were choked and his lungs were not receiving enough oxygen. We managed to resuscitate him somehow, but it took a lot of effort and time. The throat surgeon had to perform a tracheostomy on him. We were able to fix all his fractures, although he continued to remain drowsy for the next few days.

For the next four days, Shikhar was in the intensive care unit (ICU) and Sujata, his fiancé, spent her nights looking after him under the guidance of the ICU staff. I had allowed her to stay as per her request. 'I cannot stay away from him, doctor,' she had said, imploring me to allow her to keep him company.

Sujata and Shikhar had gotten engaged earlier that year on the auspicious occasion of Akshaya Tritiya. The wedding was scheduled for Valentine's Day the following year.

Even after such a major mishap, I found that Sujata was very positive throughout, as compared to Shikhar's other family members.

On my morning rounds I would find her sleeping with her head tilted awkwardly on the steel bar of the bed. Seeing me, she would quickly wake up but her eyes would be swollen. 'You should get some rest too, Sujata. Go home, you need it.' She would smile as I told her this. I clearly remember the moment when we were taking Shikhar to the operation theatre. She was sobbing terribly, eyes red with tears. She folded her hands and said, 'We've been together since school days, doctor. If he leaves me, I will die too.'

Shikhar started opening his eyes after a few days and, when the danger to his health had passed, even his tracheostomy tube was removed. In the ensuing week, I warned the family about his still-precarious situation. I told them that he had had a narrow escape and barely survived. I also informed them that recovery would be slow. I added that he had to avoid alcohol at all costs.

His mother said, 'Doctor he is on antidepressants as well.' 'Ok,' I nodded. 'Since how long? And why is he on antidepressants to begin with?' Neither of them responded and I didn't persist. I thought it best to leave such matters to the psychiatrist. Still, on hearing this, I noticed Sujata's brows had drawn together, and she had a perplexed expression on her face. Still, I decided not to dig any further.

Subsequently, Shikhar underwent a few more surgeries. Following that, and over time, his health improved but his temperament remained the same. In between surgeries, I noticed that there was a strange tension between the two families, which was made more prominent by Sujata's absence. I met Shikhar's grandmother one day. I believe she was one of the few people who understood him.

'You are like my son doctor, just try to make him feel a little better. He is very anxious today,' his grandma insisted.

So I went and paid a brief visit to Shikhar.

'What's wrong with you Shikhar?' I asked him. 'Nothing, a mild headache', he said.

'You're worrying about something, right?'

'No, I will let you know,' he said dismissively.

'You're getting discharged tomorrow by the way, so you and Sujata can finally meet.' I tried to lighten his mood.

It was getting late, so I took my leave. As soon as I left his room, my phone vibrated in my pocket. I took it out quickly to check for any urgent messages. There was one from Shikhar.

The message read:

I could only hear the blaring sirens of my own despair.
pursuits to meet her have gone astray.
trials that shall end today.

His poetic way of expressing his agony surprised me.
'Everything is finished doctor, not joking.'
'Not yet, you have to endure it. You are depressed, so

you're not thinking clearly,' I replied hurriedly. 'Sending a doctor to help you. Wait!'

Yes. get me a Doctor With a handful of pills
Or a knife
A lasso would do too.
Extreme heights
They look so tempting
Stand on the edge
And just a slip.
Where my finger
Over a lighter
Can blow me apart
Out of this existence.
I wanna say goodbye
Before today's goodnight.

'Hey, please don't say that!' He was really scaring me now. 'Hold on a bit more. Someone will tend to you soon.'

Well, I tested too
A high speed bike
For muting my agony
Executing my destiny.
But the Devil
He brought my body
To this gloomy place
Under bright lights
In a hospital gown
Tubes, tests,

Doctors pinning me down
So many voices asking me why
Why did I want to die?
On a cot with side rails
My hands felt clammy
My nerves fluttering
But now I'm learning
How to suffer with a smile.

His psychiatrist had prescribed heavy antidepressants for him. Two days later, a sleepy Shikhar got discharged, and his parents were the only ones present at the time. Sujata was conspicuous by her absence.

November 2017

Shikhar was less communicative in his initial follow-ups but gradually opened up and started questioning his future and his marriage.

'Should we postpone the wedding for a few months? Will I be able to drive? How much can I walk now? Would I be able to squat? Can I drink occasionally? I hope my memory remains intact.' He expressed these and several other doubts to me.

'I am pretty confident about Sujata, she will not leave me. What do you think doctor?'

As a matter of fact, Sujata's family was well known to me.

Shikhar had done his Masters in Economics from Delhi and was interested in studying further but his parents wanted him to join the family business, which he didn't have any liking for. It required a lot of socialising and staying up late at nights which he didn't have an appetite for. After some persuasion, he had finally started working for the family business, albeit against his wishes.

'I started socialising with rich people, but I could not forget my childhood friends. Just because they are not from elite backgrounds, doesn't mean they are not important to me. My parents have never understood that, nor does Sujata,' he told me wistfully one day.

'I grew up in a business background, without books, without art. No one around me wrote poetry or even read it. They just got their degrees, worked hard to earn money and worked even harder to multiply it. Gradually, they joined the "elite class",' Shikhar added.

'They wanted the same for me,' he said.

'As for me, I always wanted total freedom to be myself. According to me, real love is about letting a person be who they really are. And one thing is clear, I do not think like them.'

December 2017, First Week

One afternoon, I got a message from Shikhar:

'Hey doctor, I hope you have been well. Wanted to talk to you about something personal. If you could spare half an hour, I'd be grateful.'

'Please come over. Will be free by late evening,' I replied. 'We can discuss your problems over a cup of tea.'

'Dear doc, I don't drink tea. And I can't talk about happy

things either', he replied.

'Then you're missing out! Start enjoying tea and be happy', I wrote back.

But even after taking an appointment with me, Shikhar didn't turn up.

December 2017, Second Week

I was about to wrap up my OPD timings for the day when Shikhar arrived. It was a cold winter Sunday. As there were only a few appointments, I wanted to leave early.

'Sorry doctor, I got late,' Shikhar said with a small sigh.

'I think you owe me an apology, Mr Shikhar. Where have you been?' I asked, inquisitive.

'No follow-ups?' Though I started authoritatively, I couldn't help but smile back at his friendly face, and ask 'So, are you ready for a new life?'

'Yes, here I am Doc! It has only been a month…surviving. So that's truly a great feeling,' he began timidly. 'But I still continue to dwell in the past. You know, I spent this entire month alone. I've forgotten what it means to be loved, to be cared for.'

'That's quite poetic of you Shikhar. Not talking to Sujata, am I right?' I queried.

'No, keeping quiet,' Shikhar's usually stoic eyes became moist all of a sudden. There was a glimmer of doubt in them.

I didn't ask, but looked at his face, unable to decipher his thoughts.

'Yes doc, I'm keeping quiet. Haven't you heard about

'Keeping Quiet'? It's a poem written by Pablo Neruda. He requests everyone to not speak, as language creates barriers between people. So I'm keeping quiet doc.' I looked at him, wondering what might follow this admission.

'You see doc, this is an infuriating, ridiculous world of double standards,' he continued. 'I can stay out the whole night, drink and party and no one will object as long as I'm in the company of the privileged. However, the same would not be tolerated if I happened to be spending time with my childhood friends.' Why is the same reckless behaviour dismissed as 'habits' in high society?'

'See, Shikhar, binge drinking has made you anxious, society doesn't matter here,' I said interrupting his rant. 'Do you think I will allow you to drink? At least not until you're going through my treatment. And especially not after how you almost lost your life due to the accident that happened because of this, right?' I admonished him firmly.

'Okay sir, I will not!' Shikhar humbly accepted my admonition.

'Don't you like socialising doctor? You are too boring to have as a friend,' he chuckled sarcastically and got up to leave.

'Hey where are you going? Tell me about your health, at least,' I urged.

'Just wanted to see you doc, I'm doing good. Moreover, I seem to have wasted your precious evening for nothing.'

I just smiled.

'But I'd like to tell you one thing doc. I hadn't had much to drink that day, at least not as much as I usually did.'

'So how did your accident happen?' I asked with a smirk.

'Well…all in good time doc. You see, it's something complicated.'

'What?'

'Yes.'

For a moment I merely looked at him, but he was unreadable. Suddenly he opened the door and left. And, just like that, he was gone without any explanation. I watched him leave through the glass door. His prescription was still on my table.

December 2017, Third Week

One day, a familiar face hesitantly entered my cabin.

'Oh! I wasn't expecting you. Where is Shikhar?' I asked.

'He's not here,' Sujata replied.

'Hope everything is fine with him.'

'Yes,' she smiled. 'If you don't mind doctor, can I ask you something personal?'

'Sure, go ahead.'

'Thank you, doctor. Thanks for crossing the boundaries of professionalism and mentoring Shikhar emotionally, besides treating him.'

'It's fine, really.' I comforted her.

'He was able to confide in me, that's why I could do that. Now tell me what is it that's really bothering you?' I asked gently.

'Despite his recovery, my family is not sure if I should marry him,' Sujata began hesitantly.

'They have their doubts if he will ever completely give

up drinking. They want to be sure that he will never end up in the hospital again.' She continued. 'All the worries aside, I must also accept the fact that despite his dark past and habits, he has always been very caring for me and my future. He promised to love, honour and obey me from the very first day.'

'Great! What more could you want from a partner?' I asked.

'Previously it was not apparent, but my family's reluctance is clear now after the accident. It was always there, but masked under Shikhar's family's affluence. How will I get through this dilemma doc?'

'At this point, your dilemma will only lead to more doubts,' I said.

'You see doctor, I just want to make sure that he will stay by my side for a long time.'

'He will. Yet one thing is for sure, that he lives in another dimension and doesn't have space in his heart for things that have no soul. Stay on if you are sure about his love for you.' I advised her.

She left, perhaps satisfied with my answers.

Just two days later, Shikhar's mother came to see me as she had some pain in her knee.

'Sujata convinced her family to marry Shikhar in the end, thanks to your kind words for him,' she told me.

Christmas / New Year

That evening, it wasn't just any ordinary work day. It was Christmas evening, and I wanted to leave the clinic a little early. My car was already at the gate when I saw Sujata coming out of another car, limping. I had to take her for an X-ray.

I heard a familiar voice behind me. 'See doc, she has broken her ankle. Now tell her not to go to Goa. She wants to celebrate the New Year there', said Shikhar.

'Where have you been?,' I asked, pleasantly surprised to see them together.

Sujata answered, 'Doctor there has been a little too much to celebrate of late. That's why I want to go to Goa. Please let me go.' She just had a minor sprain so I bandaged her foot and prescribed some medicines. They left quickly thereafter.

February 2018

Due to my hectic schedule, I started keeping a diary in my drawer to remember all the important dates, and that evening when I opened the drawer, I caught a glimpse of a wedding card for 14 February.

Sujata's mother had come to invite me, I was informed in my office. She had left the card at the reception as there had been a lot of patients waiting to see me.

I was genuinely happy to see the wedding invite. I would certainly attend, I decided. Shikhar was finally getting married!

So, I took the card out and decided to write him a congratulatory message.

'Dear Shikhar,

Your wedding day will come and go, but may your love forever grow.

But ... I stopped myself abruptly from sending the text.

Shikhar's name was not on the wedding card. I erased the text immediately, when I realised that Sujata was marrying someone else!

I typed a new text instead:

'Dear Shikhar,

Hope you don't give up because of one bad chapter in your life. Keep going. Your story doesn't end here.'

Exactly a week later Shikhar answered:

'Hope you have been good as ever doc; thanks again for inspiring a fool.

So I am not a broken heart

I am not the weight I lost or the miles I ran.

And I am not the way I slept on my doorstep,

Under the bare sky in smell of tears and whiskey.

And I am not sitting for hours in the shower anymore.

These lines are not mine doc, it's from

'You're Doing Just Fine' and I'm just letting you know that I'm doing great doc.

And I have a girlfriend too

Living in Delhi

And my life is without blue

Thank you.'

That was the last day I received any poem or text from him. Later on, I got to know that he had given up writing, meeting his old childhood friends and had started working with his parents. I couldn't help but wonder whether it was because he had lost the love of his life or lost the life he loved. Perhaps it was both.

Annihilation

Mrs Gupta pulled out a bundle of prescriptions from her leather clutch bag. Neha, her daughter looked a little breathless and was hesitant to speak about her illness at first. Once she felt comfortable, she said, 'I felt a little better today and so they brought me to your hospital. I have been suffering for the past ten years.'

He mother interjected, 'Her whole body is in pain. She has been suffering from psychological problems as well since the past decade. We've spent a lot of money on her treatment but it seems as if it has all been wasted.'

Neha looked crestfallen and said, 'Doctor, I am tired of my mother's attitude towards me. She always makes me feel like the most useless and unwanted person in the house even though I try and help her with all the household chores.'

I was listening to both of them arguing, helplessly.

Mrs Gupta said, 'I cannot tell you, doctor, how expensive her treatment has been for us.'

On hearing her mother complain Neha could not keep

quiet and tried to explain her side of the story. She said, 'Doctor, please listen to me. I know how important an education and a career is. My academic record in my junior classes was a distinguished one. I suffered a major setback when I was in the 12th standard and because of that I could not clear the engineering entrance exam. That was ten years ago. Even today, at the age of 27, I am studying. I am pursuing an MCA (Master of Computer Application) degree from Noida. I am in competition with nobody but myself. I will not quit studying till I am physically able to.'

Neha then went on to tell me about her past and present state of affairs. 'With my class 12 examinations approaching I had started getting restless, irritable, and anxious. I feared I would not be able to take my exams. I imagined myself going through panic attacks in the examination hall but my mother kept encouraging me and I passed my exams. My mother took all the credit for it. When I failed my engineering entrance exam I was disheartened. My future looked bleak and unsure. I was weighed down by my own emotional stress. I tried to hurt myself too. I was diagnosed with PTSD, post-traumatic stress disorder (PTSD) and was prescribed anti-depressants. My parents were not satisfied with the doctor so we changed one doctor after another. Each one gave a different diagnosis. I felt miserable.'

'How are you feeling nowadays,' I asked gently.

Neha said, 'I have pain all over my body. I cannot stand for too long. Cooking is an effort. The mornings are especially difficult. These last two years have been a living hell. Maybe I am suffering from a mental illness as well.'

I asked her, 'How long have you been feeling like this?'

Neha replied, 'When I was in my late teens I often got bullied in school. There were rumours about my elder sister that affected me. For months, I would not talk to anyone outside my immediate family. At school I felt more and more isolated. My life at home was just as difficult. My mind was clouded with confusion. I could not differentiate between real and unreal. After my 12th grade examinations, I started experiencing strange symptoms. I began to feel paranoid about my mother. I feared that she was talking about me to my father and my relatives. I got depressed, to the extent so that at one point of time I refused to even get out of my bed or get dressed. I could not understand what was going on. My own words would not make sense to me. I started to hear voices in my head. My thoughts became irrational and I felt very emotional and lonely.'

Neha had my complete attention now.

'For the most part of my twenties I was really unwell. I would spend most of my time in bed shutting the world out. On a good day I would go out and meet friends, but those good days were rapidly becoming scarce. I was spending more and more time at home, trapped with these strange voices in my head. Doctor, I spent a lot of time feeling guilty about things that could not possibly have been my fault. I would blame myself for every little mishap that occurred. Sometimes I thought that if I left my bed, it might cause the death of someone in my family so I would curl up like a ball and try to stay really still for days. Finally, I was diagnosed with schizophrenia.'

I nodded understandingly.

Neha went on to say, 'This illness can make you feel confused about reality, see things that aren't there, hear voices that other people cannot hear.'

I asked the young woman, 'Have you been treated for it?' 'Not very regularly,' Neha replied.

I looked at the sheets of papers in front of me. I was actually looking for a proper diagnosis for her physical symptoms. The papers she was carrying were papers labelled with terms like 'Schizoaffective Disorder', 'Post-Traumatic Stress Disorder', 'Unstable Personality Disorder', 'Munchausen Syndrome' which is a mental disorder in which the patient fakes his or her illness to gain attention and sympathy.

I am an orthopaedic doctor. I did not have the requisite knowledge of these psychiatric illnesses.

While turning these papers over, my gaze fell on a lab report that showed that she was HLA B 27 positive.

Now I knew why she was at my clinic. I told Neha, 'Well, it is arthritis.' 'No! My limbs are okay.' She interrupted.

I knew her mental state by now so I tried to explain gently, 'It is Ankylosing Spondylitis, aka AS. It affects the spine and the large joints. Don't you feel stiff?'

Neha said.' Yes, very stiff, I told you my mornings are really bad.'

As a doctor I guessed that she might have some kind of anxiety neurosis because of this disabling arthritis. I was sure that Neha had arthritis and her problems were related to this undiagnosed illness.

It was common for patients with anxiety to get wrongly

diagnosed with schizophrenia in their teens and twenties instead of AS.

'Do you mean she doesn't have a mental problem? 'asked her mother, after I informed them of my diagnosis.

I hastened to calm her down. 'No, I am not the right person to diagnose or discard her mental illness, but one thing I can say with certainty is that she is suffering from AS. Just look at her back, it is so stiff.'

Neha's mother was not convinced and asked, 'Then why did she attempt suicide?'

She was most dismissive of any other diagnosis and strictly adhered to her belief that her daughter had schizophrenia. She started showing me prescriptions with the same psychiatric terms written on them.

I was experienced enough to handle such an over-claim of disease syndrome. Patients want sympathy and treatment, for everything they perceive to be their own correct diagnosis. I agreed with Neha about her mental illness but told her that she had arthritis as well. I wrote a prescription for her and sent her to the physiotherapist.

Neha left my chamber. She seemed confused. 'Was she suicidal?' I thought to myself.

Later in the day, I checked with my physiotherapist, John. He said, 'She is very stiff, definitely a neglected case. She didn't know about her condition so she has not had any treatment for it. She was very pleasant and spoke endlessly about her love for shopping.'

What a strange girl, I thought to myself.

That same evening Neha sent me a text message.

'Dear sir,

It seems you didn't read my note. Please read it. What I have been suffering from is Factitious disorder and not schizophrenia. The whole world (including my family) wants to believe it is schizophrenia, which is a serious mental illness. Sorry for arguing with my mother today. Doctor, I no longer feel like taking any social responsibility or continuing my studies.

Still I'm trying to learn how to deal with my sickness every day. I can still do things for myself. I like my independence, but sometimes I may need your help.

Don't take it to be a weakness or that I'm giving up. I'm trying my best.

Please read my earlier mails to you as well.

Thank You'

I now went through all the emails she had sent me. I was keen to understand Neha.

'Dear doctor,

Your hospital at Bareilly was one that I had heard of, but have not been able to get an appointment. Hope to get an appointment very soon.

I thought I would brief you on my situation. It's very personal. So I thought it would be better to write to you.'

I learnt from her trail of mails that she was a 27-year-old unmarried girl living in a middle-class joint family. She had been admitted to a hospital nine years ago following a suicide attempt, which was triggered by her failing in the engineering entrance examinations.

She came from a dysfunctional family. When she was 15,

her elder sister eloped with a Muslim boy, and had not kept in touch with the family. The family of that Muslim boy was assaulted and their house ransacked. Since then, she had been visiting a psychiatrist and was being treated for depression.

From her communication I could decipher that her authoritarian father had anankastic traits (arising from compulsion, especially in an obsessive or compulsive neurosis). Neha's mother was very critical and often even mean to her.

The family, which consisted of her parents, a brother, his daughter and her younger sister lived in a two-room set. Her room was the tiny drawing room.

Her parents had an unhappy marriage. She had been for a personality assessment by the International Personality Disorder Evaluation team at AIIMS. It was reported that she had an emotionally unstable personality disorder (impulsive type) with anxious traits. She was preoccupied with sex, but had poor reality orientation and conflicts, terms she never understood.

What I could understand from her communications was that her inner and outer hostilities began after failing the engineering entrance. She started experiencing auditory hallucinations. She tried to commit suicide by cutting her wrists.

Neha later mentioned Krishna in her emails. Krishna was a paramedic student from the medical college in her neighbourhood. He was the one who brought her to the hospital after her suicide attempt. He was a decent, handsome young man and she had grown very fond of him. Krishna and Neha would speak to each other over the phone, even during her hospitalisation. Within a week of admission, Neha's condition improved. She started to rely heavily on Krishna and their friendship grew over time.

Soon Neha was back home but now she had to confront fresh challenges. She was idle most of the time. She had slowly become habituated to lying on the bed. Her symptoms started worsening and she was diagnosed with schizophrenia. Her parents were helpless and couldn't come to terms with her condition. Krishna was the only one who doubted the diagnosis and stayed by Neha's side. Aided by medication she started pursuing her graduation. She would often meet Krishna. One day, Krishna's father suffered a stroke and he had to divide his time between his job and taking care of his father. As a result, he couldn't see Neha often.

Neha started to feel a sense of loss and deprivation. Any delay on Krishna's part in promptly replying to Neha's calls and messages would make her miserable.

Neha's parents were now completely dependent on Krishna for everything related to her hospitalisation and treatment.

He took leave from his college to take care of Neha.

In the course of the hospitalisation Neha had suffered from transient blindness for twelve hours. The ophthalmological examination did not reveal any abnormality. She kept imagining Krishna's presence in the room. She could not differentiate between reality and hallucination.

She was spinning in a vortex of mixed feelings between sorrow, desire, fear, desperation, and affection, the likes of which she had never experienced before. She was relying on Krishna to comfort her in her hour of need.

Neha had started chewing *zarda* powder (tobacco). One night, she vomited what looked like blood. The family was frightened and Krishna was summoned to administer her medication. On Neha's insistence he stayed through the night.

Neha had been put through medical questioning. It was noted that she had given inconsistent information regarding the duration, frequency and intensity of her symptoms. She was taken for supportive psychotherapy during which she revealed her inner conflicts. Since the age of eleven she had frequently seen her father forcing her mother to have sex with him and her mother being irritable the next day. She would get very distressed. She was very angry with her father and wanted to protect her mother from him.

According to Neha, it was after undergoing a stable therapeutic treatment that she confessed to Krishna that she had been lying about hearing voices in her head. She had also feigned the 'loss of vision' and 'seizure' in the past. It was actually to see Krishna and get his attention.

Neha had also noticed a change in her parents' behaviour towards her. In their distress and worry, they gave in to all her demands. They were inviting Krishna home regularly.

During the psychotherapeutic ventilation sessions, Neha displayed symptoms and behaviour that would get her the attention of her parents and her boyfriend. Adopting the 'sick role' actually fulfilled her biggest psychological need of meeting Krishna.

Neha's medication was reduced gradually and, later,

stopped altogether. Her diagnosis was revised to factitious disorder (predominantly psychological signs and symptoms) along with an emotionally unstable personality disorder of an impulsive type. She was then taken for supportive psychotherapy on a weekly basis. For the next two years, she did well without any medication. She also joined a professional MCA programme (Master of Computer Application). This was the time that she came to my clinic.

Neha's desire for Krishna grew stronger and she started feigning medical excuses to see him. She would complain of severe back aches or fake panic attacks just so that he would be summoned to her house. Their love affair continued unabated. They decided to get married and Krishna accepted her whole heartedly with all her physical limitations. Neha had never received so much support, love and, most importantly, acceptance from anyone else before.

Her happiness did not last long. One day Neha's brother, unexpectedly returned early from a wedding ceremony and caught Neha and Krishna together in her room. He lost all his composure and control. He grabbed Neha by the hair and threw her across the drawing room floor. She fainted and was so badly injured that she needed hospitalisation. Krishna was sent to jail under the Indian Penal code (IPC) Section 354.

Many months later, she came to see me. She said 'I'm awake but nightmares continue to torment me. They are endless. I keep chastising myself for being weak and worthless. My chest and heart feel very heavy. My anxiety levels are the highest they have ever been. Doctor, the sole aim in life now is to get Krishna back. Doctor, please can you help me in getting Krishna out of jail? He has been there for eight months already. No one cares about him. If you can get him released from prison I will be eternally grateful to you. Doctor, Krishna's voice rings in my ear. The winds carry his sound to me. Please help me doctor, please.'

Unfortunately, my professional limitations do not allow me to get involved in my patients' personal lives.

A month later an insurance agent came to see me in my clinic. He said, 'Do you remember treating a lady by the name of Miss Neha Gupta?'

He informed me that Neha's family had submitted some papers related to her treatment, along with a certificate which had been issued by me.

'Yes, Neha Gupta's diagnosis was clear. She had come to me for the treatment of her arthritis.' I replied calmly.

He then went on to ask me, 'Was she mentally stable?'

I counter-questioned him 'Did I mention anywhere in my report that she was mentally unstable?'

I re-read my prescription, which only had drugs for arthritis.

'See, her case was only of AS, Ankylosing Spondylitis (a form of spinal arthritis that eventually causes ankylosis of vertebral and sacroiliac joints). Anyway, why do you want to know about her mental health?' I asked.

The man informed me, 'I'm working for the 'Life Insurance Corporation (LIC)'. The family has submitted a claim.'

I asked, 'What is their claim?'

'She committed suicide!' the LIC agent informed me.

'What?' I was shocked.

The LIC agent went on to tell me, 'Yes, if she (Neha Gupta) had been suffering from a mental illness, as we have been informed, then her claim will be rejected.'

I was dumbfounded. I asked the LIC agent to email me his queries. I needed time to absorb the news and reflect on it.

If they could confirm that she had been suffering from a mental illness her claim would be rejected.

I went upstairs and stared out of the glass window, thinking to myself, 'why did you quit? What could be the reason? You said you won't quit studying, until you were physically able.'

What could be the reason? Several questions raced in my mind… schizophrenia? ankylosing spondylitis? Was it the financial burden her illness had put on the family? Was it her guilt and helplessness for not being able to stand up for the only person who had loved her unconditionally? Had she lost all hope?

Had it all been just too much for her?

As I looked across at the traffic to my right, every vehicle seemed different, some old, some new, some bright, some rusty, some large, some small but all of them were stuck in a traffic jam.

Everyone was driving to their own world, going their own way and here I was watching it all as the observer.

We are born with a strong survival instinct, so how can anyone, who hasn't gone through the pain, understand someone's wish to die?

Then, looking at the traffic jam again, I realised that this day was no different from any other.

People are born, people die, but life continues.

The next day, in my mail to the agent I firmly wrote that to the best of my knowledge Neha was suffering from arthritis and nothing else.

The Horrific Summer of 2020

The Beginning

'There are numerous ways in which God can make us
lonely and lead us back to ourselves. This is the way He
dealt with me at the time. It was like a bad dream.'
—Hermann Hesse,
Demian: Die Geschichte von Emil Sinclairs Jugend
(*Demian: The Story of Emil Sinclair's Youth*)

I remember it being 14 March 2020, when I was driving home
after an entire night of work and surgeries, in the wee hours
of the morning. As usual, the world around me slept, and
the empty roads of my small town accompanied me home.

The night is my favourite time to work in the operating
room. The tranquility of the end of the day lures everyone's
focus towards the task at hand. A weird yet calm energy flows
throughout the room as we work with amazing concentration
without any distractions.

The same goes for the streets of Bareilly at night—the city in the Indian state of Uttar Pradesh that I call home. The drive back home is quite short, so I don't get to absorb the environment to the fullest, but I'm infatuated with the desolated streets. Sometimes, it feels like they've been deserted for centuries.

That night was just the same. With the hint of a breeze and yellowing leaves swirling on the streets, the moment seemed even more peaceful. Sometimes, the view seems to be specially made for a handful of privileged people like me.

At times like these, you could be forgiven for thinking that nothing could possibly disrupt such an intimate and peaceful moment. But something did. Something non trivial. A thought that triggered an alarm, forcing my mind to descend into the pit of doubt and speculation.

A disease. A disease that seemed to be running wild from cities to towns around the world. A disease that didn't discriminate. A disease that continues to be on everyone's lips all these months later. A disease that strips us of the human touch and intimacy. A disease that chains us to our safe shelters like animals.

The same disease that I feared that night would eventually land in India. But first, I must mention a friend here, who was far, far away from my night-time driving reverie—one who was already fighting a battle that was yet to begin for us.

Piece of my Peace

It was four days after my night-time reverie, while driving home from work, on 18 March 2019, that I realised I would not be able to make it to the Madrid Trauma Conference. I had been looking forward to meeting my Swiss friend, Silvan Pasquinelli. We had met at the Davos conference in December 2019 and had become good friends, discussing orthopaedic cases and whatnot. My flight was scheduled for a month later, in mid-April—a plan that was now clearly out the window.

The first confirmed death due to Corona virus in India had already been reported.

I found myself wondering about Silvan's upcoming birthday on 20 March 2020, and how he was going to celebrate it, on duty looking after Covid-19 patients. He soon told me all about what was going on at his end of the world via email, excerpts of which I would like to share here, almost *ad verbatim*:

'Hey Brijeshwar! Sorry for not writing back for a while, kind of crazy right now but doing okay so far. Hope you're doing well too. Thank you so much for your thoughts and messages.

For the last few weeks, the news has been all about Covid-19 and its impact beyond Wuhan. Just a few weeks ago, in fact, the first case reports surfaced in our county. Overnight, the preparations to deal with this have leapt up a notch. Many are now bound to work from home, while students will continue their classes online. People who usually go out e-mailed us regarding steps to minimise transmission.

Like most of you, however, by caring for the sick, I am virtually certain to be exposed. There is no other option available at this moment either.

The death toll from the virus surpassed 5,000 in Europe today, the new epicentre of the pandemic, as Italy, Germany and Spain reported a steep rise in infections. Italy has announced the biggest day-to-day increase in the country's four-week epidemic, a day after surpassing China's death toll. The total number of deaths in Italy has reached 4,000.

I'm not gonna lie, it's scary as hell to be a resident doctor right now. In Italy, our projected immediate future, is that up to 10 per cent of infected people are going to be health care workers. They are also more likely to experience severe and critical diseases. There's not a great explanation for why this is the case other than just being at higher risk from repeated exposure to infected persons.

When we go to evaluate a patient, we can't even be sure who is infected, due to 5 percent of cases being asymptomatic carriers and the failure of our testing systems in Europe to actually diagnose people with the infection. So every time we see a patient, it is basically a game of Russian Roulette when it comes to getting exposed to the virus.

I'm not as scared for myself individually, but more for all of us health care workers as a whole. So many of us have given our entire lives to medicine; trust us, we have the loans and emotional scars to prove it. It feels scary to know that just doing our jobs during this pandemic could ultimately lead to our demise. Yes, we run that risk every day, in any call, as infections as common as the flu can still kill you, but those risks are so much greater when facing a new kind of virus, the likes of which we have never seen before in our lifetime.

But the thing is that this is nothing new. Our work exposes us to so much more. And honestly, I think that the fallout from Covid-19, while immediate and concrete, is, in many ways, similar to the other risks we run. By virtue of our commitment to humanity, we encounter an array of injuries that can impact our health, joy and longevity.

This pandemic is not a sprint, it's a marathon, and we need to be prepared now, as well as for the future.

Thank you again, and I'm glad to know a friend like you.

Stay safe,

Silvan

His revelation of the situation he was dealing with didn't just scare me, but left me speechless over his show of courage. And that only prompted me to offer him a piece of my peace.

I wrote back:

'Dragging through the mud and scum of these crazy times
You walk into the hospital corridors like a soldier
You stay there, work there, eat there and sleep there
You do that and then you put your life out there too
Juggling, day in and day out
Night after night
You hope for the best and you hold it like a light within you
If you do all this and you do so without breaking a sweat
Then you can make things happen almost like magic.

Silvan Pasquinelli, you are part of a remarkable story of human courage and the triumph of the human spirit. You are a part of history in the making.

Amid this crisis, good news is happening.

Happy birthday dear Silvan!

✺

Corresponding with Silvan brought me back to my own reality, back home in India. What would happen to my nights? I wondered. Will my days and nights dissolve into one? Will this tranquility of the darkness hold the same charm once the disease took hold and added my small town to ghost cities around the world?

The fear that these silent trees, the gentle breeze and the peaceful quiet could exist at a time other than the dark of the night, was enough to jerk me awake from my reverie that morning. Only to lead my thoughts from worrying about an uncertain future, to way back into the past.

Virus *katha*

Illness was once considered a curse of the gods or various wrathful deities, or so we believed. Most of my childhood was spent in absolute cluelessness about any sort of disease pathology or mechanism. The reasoning was rather simple and quite unlike what* would want us to believe. My grannies, mother and various aunts would often opine that an angry

---

*Robbin's

goddess had cast a spell that had somehow translated into a fever that kept me in bed. The cure, though, was strikingly simple even then. Apart from a few theatrics in the temple or inside the designated prayer room of the house, multiple baths and hygiene were considered paramount in a patient's fight against the apparent 'intruder'. The concept of 'spreading through touch' ruled the roost.

The emergence of Covid-19 and its crippling devastation has served as a reminder of how those old and simple techniques are once again at the forefront of the thin line separating disease from health. Naturally, the current situation has made me spare more than a thought about those sweet ladies from my childhood. How would they have dealt with this monster?

Would it be the usual algorithm of clean clothes, praying, fasting and chanting the *Ramayana* all day, to heal us, like it was all a big bad eclipse? Perhaps.

The difference is that now, after all these years, I have finally understood—in painstakingly intricate detail— about what a virus is. In the simplest of terms, it is just an infinitesimal particle of protein. With fancy names like Zika, Nipah, Ebola, Rubella, it has a near-lethal ability to enslave the very origin of human existence inside the genome. The DNA, hallucinating on behalf of its master—the virus— obeys its orders blindly, producing even more of the virus in the host.

No matter how much progress humans make, nature remains forever more powerful. And, until a few months ago, we hadn't even come up against anything like Covid-19, at least in our lifetimes. It has turned the world on its head in a matter of months, and has swept into our lives in a very weird and intrusive manner. This invisible enemy can wipe out half of humanity like the villainous Thanos does in *The Avengers* movies and comic books.

Even the so-called superpowers must surrender to its might, and re-direct resources from large industrial projects to make the humble mask, and give a leg up to pharmaceutical factories instead of mass-producing weapons of war. All the while, health workers are working tirelessly, at great risk to their families back home, to save lives, without taking a break and by continuing to put themselves in harm's way. The fight to discover a vaccine is on.

Where exactly did we go wrong?

We were not prepared for this. No one was. Now we stand, shoulder to shoulder in worry, fearful for our most vulnerable patients, friends, family, colleagues, as well as healthcare and other frontline workers. And standing in the midst of some unprecedently difficult choices, some of us have given up our own lives to it. But it does not seem ready to stop, or even slow down to let us catch a much-needed breath.

In the meantime, the largest-ever global lockdown has ended, even as India braces for what might come next. Experts say loosening the restrictions might mean that new cases will increase at faster rates, which, in turn, will intensify pressure on hospitals that are already under immense strain—and will affect overall access to healthcare.

Months of living under the shadow of the Corona virus often makes me wonder what else is in store for us in the months to come. It is a long and dark tunnel, for sure, where the weak and unprivileged among us may be unable to walk much further, unless help is at hand.

On the other hand, over the past few months, I have witnessed truly unparalleled bravery and resourcefulness all around me, as the world comes together to fight. We *will* survive this and the globe *will* awaken from this nightmare to a world where Mother Nature will be waiting for us with a smile. I thank all my comrades on the frontlines. You all were, are and forever will be my true superheroes.

So, this is not just my story. This is a story of countless frontline workers that the entire world is depending on. This is a story of warriors who won't receive medals for their bravery or popularity. Their stories, however, will go down in the annals of history. Each story, with its own ebbs and flows, will be treasured, for years to come, by those who have borne witness to it. Including me. And for their service, all of humanity will be forever indebted and grateful.

War of the virus

As I continue driving to and from work, via what are now eerily deserted streets, other frontline professionals, in this strange and fierce war on the dreaded virus, are hard at work. I often imagine how others' days and nights might look, and I have been fortunate to bear witness to two such stories.

Papa Giovanni XXIII Hospital, Bergamo, Italy

Annalisa is tired. It's five in the morning and she's at work again. A peaceful cup of morning coffee and looking presentable for a new work day are luxuries she has long forgotten.

Days and nights have suddenly become the same. There is no time to glance at the watch; no use in trying either, because it's covered with gloves that are changed constantly throughout the day.

She washes her hands all day long, and changing gloves after gloves is all she knows now. The creases on her face are hidden under the extensive armour of her PPE suit and head shield.

Every morning, she and her colleagues are there, almost as if ready to go to war—like soldiers banding together against a common foe.

Syringes filled with blood and medicines are doled out. Oxygen levels are checked and rechecked. X-ray plates are attached to countless sternums. Only the seriously sick patients are here. As they get better, other, sicker patients take their place.

As for those who succumb to the dreadful illness, their oxygen is saved for yet another patient and their families are duly notified. All they are given are foggy scuba diving glasses to absorb the tears. The last goodbye is not seen, it is only felt.

Annalisa's uncle, Aleksandro, had been suffering with fever for the past eleven days. He had waited for the promised ambulance every day, to no avail. In the end, he succumbed to the virus and had to bid his final farewell from home. All

Annalisa could do was shed a tear on hearing the sad news.

Everyone is racing against time, doing their best, but all you can see are ashes falling out the windows of Papa Giovanni's Hospital in Bergamo, Italy. Annalisa continues to work, even under the shadow of death. She dusts the ashes off of those who lay asleep.

Unfortunately, she hasn't been able to dust them off of herself on time.

She has tested positive.

She's not coughing but, once the fever sets in, she'll be sent home.

She is tired and wants to go home.

She's apologetic, but all she wants to do is go home.

※

National Institute of Allergies and Infectious Diseases (NIAID), Maryland, USA

As Friday comes to an end and meetings get over, it is just Kizzmekia who is still working behind closed doors. Like everyone else, she's racing against time but the catch is that she's one of the few who is trying to end it all.

The 34-year-old viral immunologist Dr Kizzmekia Corbett, is the scientific lead for the Corona Virus Vaccine Program at the Vaccine Research Center. The National Institute of Allergy and Infectious Diseases (NIAID) is one of the 27 institutes and centers that make up the National Institutes of Health (NIH), an agency of the United States Department of Health and Human Services. Dr Corbett's team studies the Corona virus. Her work, in particular, began with the Middle East Respiratory Syndrome (MERS) outbreak and now spans the Corona virus pandemic.

Being a woman of African-American descent makes her a double minority in the field of medical science. It also makes her prone to discrimination and disguised misogyny. People often underestimate her work and devotion toward the cause. One of them says on Twitter that she should be working at a burger joint instead, but she laughs it off and continues to focus on her work. She believes it will speak for itself, and her friends are already preparing for the arrival of a Nobel Prize in the future.

She is an inspiration to everyone around her, especially those who closely following her work. It's not just the anticipated results that she would eventually be given credit for, but for the current hope that she is already giving to millions around the world.

Kizzmekia has a loving family—her step brother, sisters, nephews, nieces and grandmothers are all praying for her. She is a dedicated girl. She believes in miracles, but credits science and, though the latter is her friend, Jesus is her best friend of them all.

Hope she can make it to the church this Easter. She is dedicated and devoted to her clinical trials, handling it all with grace; from data to emails, samples to calls and spreadsheets—she's doing it all.

The media has finally caught up with her work and has begun showing her the appreciation she deserves. And while we all pray for an end to this deadly virus, she is already in the deep-end of the action at the head of the research into its cure.

Kizzmekia is making a vaccine and she is making history.

ACKNOWLEDGMENTS

These stories are inspired by my patients, without whom there would be no book. When I started writing, the feedback of my colleague Dr Ashish John and my older son Anirudh helped shape these amazing stories. Anirudh, who is pursuing his final-year MBBS from KMC, Manipal, in fact went a step ahead and shared them with his entire class for their collective feedback. These two kinds of feedback—from Ashish, who knew these patients, and Anirudh and his friends, who didn't—worked in tandem and proved to be a winning combination in the end.

I would like to express my thanks to Dibakar Ghosh at Rupa Publications for his guidance and patience in seeing me through this journey. This book has been given shape by Natasha Kumar Verma, and my thanks are due to her for working on the initial draft of the manuscript. My gratitude is also due to my friend Preeti Singh for giving the final touches to this book, for her initial suggestions and the aesthetics that she brought with her editorial experience and creative suggestions.

Finally, I'd like to thank my younger son Abhimanyu and my wife Garima for their unwavering love and support.

In the end, this book is as much mine as it is of my patients and the great team of doctors that I work with. I continue to be amazed by their resilience and bravery.